* * * * * *

As Marcus rose up and started to swing his leg over his saddle, the short man reached for his gun. With one foot still in the stirrup and one hand on the saddle horn, Marcus drew his gun so fast that he had it pointed at the man's chest before the man could clear leather. The man froze.

Although the man's gun was in his hand, the end of the barrel had not cleared his holster. The man's eyes were as big as saucers and his jaw hung open from the surprise. Fearing that he was about to die, his eyes almost immediately began pleading for his life.

"I think there's been enough killing over the past few years. What would it prove if I were to kill you now?" Marcus asked, then waited for some kind of a reply.

The man stood there in silence. His heart was stuck in his throat. He was in shock at the speed Marcus had shown. His mouth was dry and his feet seemed to be frozen in place.

* * * * * *

Other Large Print Editions by J.E. Terrall

Western Short Stories
  The Old West
  The Frontier
  Untamed Land
  Frontier Justice
  Tales from the Territory

Western Novels

  Conflict in Elkhorn Valley
  The Valley Ranch War

# UNTAMED LAND

## A COLLECTION OF WESTERN SHORT STORIES

### by

### J.E. TERRALL

ISBN: 978-0-9994727-0-5

This is a work of fiction. Names, characters, and incidents are either a product of the author's imagination or are used fictitiously, and any resemblance to actual persons, living or dead, is purely coincidental.

Printed in the United States of America
Large print edition printed by createspace.com.

Front cover photo taken by the author, J.E Terrall

Book Layout/
Formating:   J.E. Terrall
             Custer, South Dakota

# UNTAMED LAND

## A COLLECTION OF
## WESTERN SHORT STORIES

To Pat and Lori Luze

# UNTAMED LAND

# THE TALL STRANGER

The Civil War was over, but not the hatred some people felt for each other. The Civil War had caused many wounds that would take a long time to heal, and there were some that would never heal. The South had been left in ruins. There were men, young and old alike, who had nothing to return to but burned out buildings and land scorched by the devastation of war.

Many of those men chose to leave the south and move west in the hope of finding a new life and put the old one behind them. Such a man was Marcus Burnard of Georgia.

Marcus was a tall, handsome southern gentleman with wavy black hair and a thin mustache. He cut a fine figure of a man in his uniform and had proven himself to be a good officer. He was also good with a gun and a deck of cards.

He had been captured after a bloody battle in North Carolina as the war was coming to an end. After his release from a Union prison camp, he returned to his father's plantation in

Georgia only to find the large southern style house had been burned to the ground. The plantation had been taken over by northern carpetbaggers. Most of the land had been sold off and the slaves were gone.

His father and sister were living in a nearby town and had adjusted to their new lifestyle. With what they had been able to hide from the carpetbaggers, they were able to open a general store.

Marcus had no desire to work in his father's general store. The last thing he wanted was to remain in Georgia with all the reminders of the war. He wanted to build a new life somewhere west of the Mississippi River. He packed up what he could, said goodbye to his father and sister, and headed west.

Two months later, Marcus found himself riding into a small town in the Dakota Territory. There were only three wooden buildings and four tents with wooden fronts that could be called businesses.

Marcus rode up in front of the hotel. It was the largest building in town. He sat on his horse while he took a minute to look around.

It had not been a town for very long, but it just might have a future, he thought. Maybe, a future for him.

He was about to get off his horse when a young woman came out on the boardwalk of the hotel. He found himself watching her every move. She was the prettiest thing he had seen in a long time.

The young woman, Jenny Taylor, had long dark brown hair that rested easily on her shoulders and framed her pretty face. Her eyes were dark brown and sparkled in the afternoon sunlight. He didn't miss the fact that she had a nice figure under the simple calico cotton dress she was wearing.

As she started to sweep off the boardwalk, she turned and looked up at him. She stopped, smiled politely, then shyly turned away to continue sweeping. It had been a long time since she had seen a man as tall and handsome, and one who sat a horse as well as the stranger did. He was different from the men who lived in the area. She hadn't missed the fact that he had been watching her, either.

As Marcus sat on his horse watching her, he noticed she would glance at him every once in awhile as she swept the boardwalk. He wondered if she might even be flirting with him just a little. He didn't mind, but right now his stomach was in need of his attention. It had been days since he had had a decent meal.

"Excuse me, Miss, but could you tell me where I might get something to eat?" he said using his best southern manners.

"You can get something to eat right here at the hotel," she replied with a pleasant smile.

Her voice was soft and pleasant. Her smile seemed to light up her face.

"No, he can't," came a booming voice from the doorway of the hotel. "We don't serve no Rebs 'round here."

The smile on Marcus's face slowly disappeared as he turned his head to look at the man. He saw a short man with broad shoulders. His build was heavy, yet muscular. He had a dirty face that was partially covered by an equally unkempt beard. The clothes the man was wearing were as dirty as the man himself. His boots were covered with dried mud and he looked as if he had just come out of the backcountry.

Marcus took note of the gun the man wore low on his hip. It was the only thing about the man that appeared to be clean. To Marcus, that was an indication of the man's ability to use it.

"Do you own this hotel, sir?" Marcus asked calmly and politely.

"No, but we don't like southern trash 'round here."

"In case you hadn't heard, mister, the War Between the States is over," Marcus said, knowing full well it didn't matter to him.

"You stay on that there horse and ride outta here while you still can."

"Mister, I don't want any trouble with you. All I want is something to eat and I intend to get it here," Marcus said slowly and clearly, his voice showing no fear.

The short man's eyes narrowed in anger. There was no doubt he was going to cause trouble. Marcus didn't want any trouble, but he had already decided that he was not leaving town on an empty stomach.

As Marcus rose up and started to swing his leg over his saddle, the short man reached for his gun. With one foot still in the stirrup and one hand on the saddle, Marcus drew his gun so fast that he had it pointed at the man's chest before the man could clear leather. The man froze.

Although the man's gun was in his hand, the end of the barrel had not cleared his holster. The man's eyes were as big as saucers and his jaw hung open from the surprise. Fearing that he was about to die, his eyes pleaded for his life.

"I think there's been enough killing over the past few years. What would it prove if I were to kill you now?" Marcus asked, then waited for some kind of a reply.

The man stood there in silence. His heart was stuck in his throat. He was in shock at the speed Marcus had shown. His mouth was dry and his feet seemed to be frozen in place.

The terror that the man felt had started to show in his face and body. His body began to tremble and sweat rolled down the man's face in spite of the fact it was a cool day. Without saying a word, the man let his gun slide back into his holster. He then raised his hands above his head.

Slowly, Marcus lowered himself to the ground. He didn't take his gun off the man, nor did he take his eyes off him as he stepped out of the saddle.

Marcus moved around from behind his horse and slowly walked up to the man. Standing directly in front of him, Marcus looked him in the eyes.

He leaned close to him and whispered, "I don't want to kill you, but I will if I ever see you again. I will not wait for you to go for your gun. I will simply shoot you on sight. Do I make myself clear?"

The man looked into Marcus's eyes and found it was not hard for him to believe Marcus could and would kill him like he said.

"Yes, sir," the man managed to mumble, his voice quivering.

"I don't want to see you again, ever. Now go away," Marcus said calmly and softly.

The man stood there for a second staring into Marcus's eyes, and then slowly started to back away. He backed up until he got to the corner of the hotel. He glanced down the alley between the buildings, and then looked back at Marcus. He wasn't sure if he should take the chance and make a run for it down the alley, or if he should keep backing up. He decided he would make a run for it and darted off the boardwalk and down the alley.

As soon as the short man was gone, Marcus slipped his gun back in his holster as smoothly as he had drawn it. He continued to watch the corner of the building in case the man decided to come back.

Marcus turned and looked along the boardwalk to where the woman had been standing. She was standing there looking at him. The expression on her face was that of someone who had suddenly discovered a friend was not who she thought him to be. She didn't even know the tall dark stranger's name. She wasn't sure she wanted to get to know him, now.

"I'm sorry, Ma'am," Marcus said politely. "I'm sorry you had to see that."

She stood silently staring into his eyes. He had seemed like the perfect gentleman. Yet, he had drawn his gun with the quickness of a professional gunfighter. In spite of it, he had not killed the man who had threatened to kill him.

She had seen men in gunfights before, but never had she seen anything like this. The tall stranger was different. She didn't know what to think. Not sure what she should do or what she should say, she turned around and hurried back inside the hotel.

Marcus watched her as she left. He was sure he had disturbed her sensibility in some way. She was young and most likely had some sort of idea what a man should be like, and he apparently didn't fit her ideals.

Marcus stood on the boardwalk for a minute before he turned and went inside the hotel. As he entered the lobby, he stopped to look around.

The hotel was a two-story building with rooms to rent on the second floor. On the main floor was the lobby that had the desk and a couple of places to sit. Off to the left of the lobby was a bar with a couple of tables where one could sit for a drink or a friendly game of cards.

To the right was another small room that had three tables. It was obviously the dining room as the tables had tablecloths over them. It was a place where a hungry person might be able to get something to eat. That was what he was looking for.

"May I help you?"

Marcus turned and looked at the man standing behind the hotel desk. The man was tall and skinny, and wore wire framed glasses that hung on his long nose which looked more like a beak. His black hair was plastered down with some kind of grease. He was wearing a wrinkled white shirt and a black vest with a black garter on each arm.

"May I help you?" the man repeated.

"Yes, sir. I would like a room for the night and a meal."

"The room will be two bits a night. The meal will be two bits also, sir," the desk clerk said without any emotion.

Marcus walked up to the desk clerk and laid down four bits. He signed the registration book.

"Is there a livery stable in town? I need a place to put up my horses."

"No, sir, but we have a stable out back where you can bed down your horses for an additional two bits. You will have to take care of them yourself. We do not provide that service," the man explained. "There's hay in the loft and grain in the barrel next to the door. Both are included in the price."

"Thank you. I'll take care of my horses before I have dinner."

"If you would like, I can have your dinner ready for you. We have steak, fried potatoes and corn with a biscuit and wild honey tonight."

"That sounds good. I'll be back in a few minutes," Marcus assured him.

Marcus went back out the front of the hotel, untied his horses and led them around back to the stable. As he did, he couldn't help but think about the desk clerk and the way he talked. He was certain the clerk was from back east somewhere, most likely from the northeast. The man appeared to be well educated as he had a good command of the English language.

After caring for his horses, Marcus went to the back door of the hotel. Next to the door was a table with a washbasin, a pitcher of water and several towels hanging next to it. He washed his hands and face and went inside.

When he got to the dining room, he found his dinner waiting for him at one of the tables. The young woman who had been out front earlier was pouring hot coffee into a cup.

"This is your place, sir," the woman said politely.

"Thank you," Marcus replied as he walked up next to the table.

He pulled out the chair and sat down. Marcus continued to watch the woman as she left the dining room. She had been polite, yet distant at the same time. Marcus felt she was probably thinking about what had happened earlier.

Marcus turned his attention to the meal that had been set for him. He discovered the food was good and began to enjoy it.

Suddenly, there was a noise at the window. Marcus responded instantly. He pushed back away from the table while at the same time he drew his gun and fired at the man in the front window as a shot rang out, breaking one of the windowpanes.

The bullet from Marcus' gun crashed through another windowpane and hit the man in the chest. The force of the bullet forced the man back against the hitching rail where he fell off the boardwalk to the ground.

As Marcus stood up and moved closer to the window, he saw the man who had challenged him earlier lying in the dirt between the boardwalk and the hitching rail. The man was dead.

There was the sound of someone running behind Marcus causing him to swing around quickly. He found himself pointing his gun at the desk clerk.

The desk clerk stopped quickly and threw his hands into the air. His eyes showed the fear he was feeling. He was sure Marcus was going to shoot him, too.

"Please, mister," the desk clerk pleaded.

"I'm not going to shoot you. You can put your hands down," Marcus said as he lowered his gun.

Marcus slowly turned and looked out the window again. People were beginning to gather on the boardwalk. A couple of them were looking in the dining room to see who had fired the shot that had killed the man in the street.

Marcus turned back and looked down at the table. The man's shot had hit the table and went right through his dinner plate. The plate had shattered and food was all over the table and on the floor.

The young woman came into the dining room and saw the mess. She looked first at the table and then at Marcus. She didn't know what had happened, but she was both glad to see the handsome stranger was not hurt, and upset because he had shot a man. She couldn't explain her mixed feelings, not even to herself.

"I'm sorry about the mess," Marcus said to the desk clerk. "I'll pay for the damages."

"We'll see what he has on him. Whatever it is, I'll apply it to the damages," the desk clerk said as he looked out the window.

Just then the town sheriff arrived. He was an older man with gray in his handlebar mustache and in his hair. He was lean of build, but looked like he would be able to handle himself in a fight.

The sheriff looked at the body lying in the dirt, then looked through the window. He could see Marcus standing next to the table with the desk clerk and Jenny standing nearby. After telling a couple of men to get the dead man off the street, he went inside the hotel.

"What's your name, young fella?" the sheriff asked as he walked into the dining room.

"Burnard, Marcus Burnard."

"You want to tell me what's this all about, Mr. Burnard?"

Marcus explained everything that had happened from the time he rode into town up to and including the shooting of the man. The sheriff listened intently.

"Anyone have anythin' to say about this?" he asked as he looked around.

"I do," Jenny said as she glanced over at Marcus before taking a step toward the sheriff.

"And what is it you have to say, Miss Jenny? Did you see the shootin'?"

"Well, no, not exactly. But I do know what Mr. Burnard said was true. Bobby Sanders tried to run him out of town because he is from the south."

The sheriff looked at Marcus for a minute before he spoke.

"You must be pretty handy with a gun to have beat Bobby Sanders to the draw. Are you a gunfighter, mister? We don't cotton to gunfighters 'round here."

"No, sir. I don't like being pushed around. The war is over and I'd just as soon forget it. I've got nothing against anyone. I want to leave the past behind and get on with my life."

"Well, young fella, that may not be so easy now."

"Why's that?"

"The man you killed has three older brothers, and I doubt they will take it kindly you killin' one of their own. Once the word gets out you killed Bobby, they will be comin' after you. I suggest you leave town now, before they have time to find out."

"Sheriff, it's your job to protect him," Jenny said.

"Now, Jenny, this is none of your concern," the sheriff said politely.

"It is my concern. It's the concern of every one of us in this town. We can't let the Sanders brothers run this town. This stranger came into town with no other purpose than to get a place to rest for the night and something to eat. If a man can't do that in peace, then this town isn't worth anything," she insisted.

"Now listen here, girl," the sheriff said, but was interrupted by Jenny.

"No, you listen. If this town isn't safe for the people who live here, then this isn't a fit place to raise a family. Didn't we move here to build a safe place to live?" Jenny asked as she looked at the people who had gathered around.

Marcus looked around. There didn't seem to be a single one of them that didn't agree with what Jenny had said. The few women who were there tended to be a little more vocal about it than the men.

"We got us a school teacher comin' soon," one of the ladies said. "If we have a town that has no laws, we won't have a school teacher long. I, for one, want my children to learn to read and write."

"That's right," another said.

"We want a safe place to live and raise a family, and we're going to have it if we got to fight to get it," another woman insisted.

"What do you want me to do against the likes of them," the sheriff asked.

"We want you to protect the people of this town, and that includes people who are ridin' through peaceable like," one of the women said.

"You can deputize every man and every woman in town if necessary to make the Sanders obey the law," another woman shouted from the back of the small crowd.

"It's time you do your job, sheriff," Jenny demanded.

Marcus and the sheriff looked over the people that had assembled inside the hotel as well as those outside. There was no doubt what the town wanted. They were not going to put up with lawlessness in their town any more.

"The way I figure it, the three of them will come into town after dark," the sheriff said thoughtfully.

"Then you best get to making some plans on how to deal with them," Jenny said with a matter fact tone in her voice.

The crowd made it clear they were not going to stand for anything less than a town that was peaceful and safe. The sheriff looked over at Marcus. He looked as if he didn't know how to handle the situation.

"Well, son, I think we need to talk."

After the sheriff picked out four men from the crowd in front of the hotel, he led them down the street to his office. While the others left, Marcus, the sheriff and the four men sat down in the sheriff's office and worked out a plan to stop the Sanders brothers from shooting up the town.

By the time darkness fell, Marcus had finally had his dinner and was sitting at a table in the bar of the hotel. He was sitting with his back in a corner so he could see anyone who came into the hotel. He could also see out the front window.

The sheriff had placed himself in the dining room. He was behind the door and out of sight from anyone who might come into the hotel. The four men he had picked from the crowd were in the two buildings directly across the street from the front of the hotel. They had rifles and shotguns and were waiting for the arrival of the Sanders brothers.

It was quiet outside. The lamps had been lit in the bar and lobby. The two lamps on either side of the front door to the hotel had also been lit for the evening. There was nothing to do now but wait. It was not a question of if the Sanders brothers would come, it was only a question of when.

Time passed slowly as the men waited. Marcus played a little solitaire while he waited.

"I think we have company," the sheriff whispered as he heard the sound of several horses approaching the hotel.

"I hear them," Marcus replied.

There was suddenly silence again as the Sanders brothers stopped at the hitching rail in front of the hotel. They sat in their saddles as they all looked around.

"A bit quiet, don't you think," Sam Sanders said as he looked at the front of the hotel.

Sam Sanders was the oldest of the brothers. He was short in stature like Bobby, but he was strong. He was also unkempt like Bobby had been.

"Yeah," Billy Sanders agreed as he looked at the store directly across the street.

"You think it's a trap?" Jimmy Sanders said, the youngest of the remaining Sanders brothers.

"Nah. This town ain't got the guts ta back up some damn Reb. He's hidin' some place. And that sheriff hasn't got the nerve to try ta do anythin' about it."

"If he's as fast as they say he is, . . . "Jimmy said, but was quickly cut off by his older brother Sam.

"There ain't no one that fast. Let's get to it."

Sam swung his leg over the saddle and stepped down off his horse. The others followed. Once they were all on the ground, they stepped up on the hotel boardwalk and looked over the town again.

"Billy, you go around back and make sure he don't get out that way."

Marcus could hear them talking, but could not understand what was being said. He could hear the sound of boots running along the boardwalk. The sound drifted away. He knew one of them was most likely going around back, probably getting ready to come in the back door.

Shortly after the sound had faded away, he heard the front door of the hotel open. He watched as two rather stocky men walked into the lobby. Neither of them had guns in their hands, but they wore their guns strapped low on their legs as if they might know how to use them.

All of the Sanders brothers thought themselves to be pretty good with a gun, Marcus thought. Marcus knew he was good, but not against all three at the same time. The odds were against him. He hoped the plan he had worked out with the sheriff was going to work.

As Sam and Jimmy Sanders stepped into the doorway between the lobby and the bar, Marcus prepared himself for a bloody shoot out. It was not what he wanted, but it was beginning to look like it was going to play out that way.

"You the Reb killed my little brother," Sam said as he glared at Marcus.

"If you mean am I the one who shot the man that tried to bushwhack me while I was sitting down to dinner, the answer is yes,"

Marcus said calmly while watching them closely.

"You callin' my brother a bushwhacker?" Sam said.

"What would you call a man who is too much of a coward to face you?" Marcus asked.

Sam seemed suddenly confused. This man didn't seem to be afraid of him. That had never happened to him before. Everyone was afraid of the Sanders brothers. And to top it off, this man had called his brother a coward and challenged him to argue the point.

Jimmy had been watching Marcus. He glanced at his big brother and wondered what was going to happen now.

"I think you should stand up," Sam said, still a little confused but seeing no other way to avenge his brother.

"Why?"

"Cause I said so," Sam yelled.

"Mr. Sanders, your brother would not be dead now if he had done what I told him. I had the perfect chance to kill him when he drew down on me, but I didn't. Instead, I told him that I never wanted to see him again. If I did, I would kill him. After I had let him go, he was stupid enough to come back and try to bushwhack me. He left me with no choice but to kill him.

"Now if you want to get out of this hotel alive, I would suggest you turn around and leave now," Marcus added.

"You're pretty damn brave," Sam said with a chuckle.

"You wouldn't think so if you knew what I know."

"And what's that?" Sam said as the grin on his face slowly faded away.

"First of all, there are four citizens of this town who have been deputized and are ready to gun you down in the street should you decide to make a fight of this," Marcus said calmly.

"The town folks ain't got the nerve," Sam said with a snicker.

"I wouldn't place any bets on that. They have had it with men like you. They are tired of putting up with you making their town an unsafe place to live. They want a nice quiet town to raise their families in, and they are ready to fight for it."

"You think that's going to stop us from killin' you?"

"That alone, maybe not. But you might consider the fact that the sheriff is standing right behind you with a double barrel shotgun, and he's ready to use it."

"I think you best listen to him, boys," the sheriff said before they could argue the point.

Sam and Jimmy slowly turned their heads and looked over their shoulders to find the sheriff standing behind them.

"Now we can play this out one of two ways. You can drop your guns and leave town peacefully, or we can have it out right now," the sheriff said.

"You think this is over?" Sam said.

"It better be. If any of you come into town with a gun, you will be shot on sight. Do I make myself clear?" the sheriff asked.

Sam looked at Jimmy. They realized they didn't have much of a choice. They slowly turned around and started toward the door.

Suddenly, there was a gunshot from the back of the lobby. It caught the sheriff off guard. The sheriff dropped his gun and fell to the floor with a gunshot wound to his arm.

Sam and Jimmy started to draw their guns as they turned around. Marcus quickly drew his gun and fired two quick shots. The first one hit Sam in the upper right side of his chest sending him spinning around and falling over one of the tables in the dining room. As he collapsed on the floor, his gun flew out of his hand and out of his reach. The expression on his face showed he had not expected to lose. His eyes quickly went blank as he died.

The second shot hit Jimmy square in the chest and sent him back up against the wall. The look on Jimmy's face was one of disbelief. He couldn't believe he had been shot, but he didn't have much time to think about it, as he was dead before he hit the floor.

There was a third shot that ripped through Marcus' side. As he doubled over in pain, he was able to get off one more shot. It was a wild shot toward his assailant. Luckily his bullet found its mark as it smashed into the stomach of the last living Sanders.

The gunfight was over in a matter of seconds. Two were dead, one was fatally wounded, and two were shot up enough to put them out of commission for at least a few days.

While Marcus and the sheriff lay on the floor wounded, the four deputies came running across the street. It was a matter of seconds before Jenny and two other women came rushing to help the wounded. Jenny ran over to Marcus.

"I'm sorry I messed up your floor," Marcus said with a grin that didn't hide the fact he was in pain.

"Be quiet," she said softly as she looked into his eyes.

Marcus looked up at her as she tore open his shirt and started to administer to his wound. It wasn't long before Marcus was carried off to his room.

It had been a while and things had calmed down in the little town. His wound had been bandaged and he had been sleeping. As he woke up, he turned his head and saw Jenny resting in a chair next to the bed. She had stayed with him, for how long he didn't know. He took a few moments to look at her. At that moment he made up his mind to settle down in this little town in the Dakota Territory.

# THE LAST PATROL

In the late fall of 1877, a U.S. Army wagon train of supplies failed to show up at Fort Meade in the Dakota Territory. A patrol was sent out in search of it. The wagon train was found some twenty miles south and east of Rapid City along Battle Creek. All the supplies were gone and all the members of the wagon train were dead, including a woman who was on her way to Fort Meade to join her husband. The patrol immediately began following the tracks left by the raiders. They headed west toward the Black Hills.

The cavalrymen moved quietly along the creek led by two experienced soldiers, Sergeant Jacob Wells and Corporal John Hayes. The rest of the patrol was made up of five regular U.S. Army Cavalrymen. They ranged in age from eighteen to forty-three, and their experience on the frontier was as varied as their ages.

One morning, after several days of tracking the raiders, the weather had turned cold and damp. A thick layer of fog covered the lowland along Battle Creek. The tension in the air was as thick as the fog.

Suddenly, Sergeant Wells raised his hand in the air. Everyone stopped and began looking around. Corporal Hayes silently moved up alongside Sergeant Wells.

"You hear somethin', Sergeant?" Corporal Hayes asked in a whisper.

"I'm not sure."

Sergeant Wells drew his rifle out of the scabbard and swung his leg over the saddle. He lowered himself down onto the ground and stood quietly next to his horse and listened. Sergeant Wells looked up at Corporal Hayes and motioned for him to dismount.

Corporal Hayes passed the word on down the line for the soldiers to dismount quietly. He then moved up next to Sergeant Wells.

"Something's over there," Sergeant Wells said. "Have Private Johnson stay with the horses. We're going to check it out."

Corporal Hayes gave the order. Each member of the patrol handed the reins of his horse to Private Johnson, drew their rifles from their scabbards, and joined the sergeant. The sergeant led them to the creek where they formed a picket line among the trees along the bank.

It was an eerie feeling being in the fog. Everything had a ghostly appearance. Even the trees didn't appear real.

"Did you hear something?" Sergeant Wells asked.

"Yeah, but I'm not sure what. It almost sounds like someone in pain."

"Check it out, but don't take any chances."

Corporal Hayes nodded and started off across the shallow creek disappearing in the fog. He began slowly working his way among the trees.

The fog limited Corporal Hayes's ability to see more than a few yards. It was like moving in a gray darkness that closed in around him, but it was a darkness no lantern would help.

Corporal Hayes stopped suddenly. Out in front of him was a hint of yellow that seemed to flicker in the fog. There was no smell of smoke, but the slight breeze was coming from behind him.

Careful not to make any sounds, he slowly moved toward the flickering light. As he grew closer, he could see it was a campfire. He hunkered down behind a tree to look around. All he saw was a bedroll near the fire. There were no other bedrolls that he could see.

The bedroll looked like there might be someone in it. He carefully worked his way around the perimeter of the campsite. After circling the entire camp, Corporal Hayes had been unable to find any signs of anyone else. There wasn't even a horse close by.

As he was about ready to leave, he heard the moaning sound again. It was coming from the bedroll. There was someone in it and he had probably been left there to die.

The thought passed through the corporal's mind that he should find out who it was in the bedroll. It could be one of those they were after. If it was, he might be able to provide information on where the others had gone. On the other hand, he could be a decoy and it could be a trap. He decided the best thing for him to do was to report back to the sergeant. After all, his assignment had been to simply check things out and report back.

As quietly as possible, Corporal Hayes withdrew from the campsite. He worked his way back through the fog and across the creek into the line of trees to the patrol. When he got there, he looked around but they were gone. He began to carefully retrace every step he had taken in his mind. He knew he had crossed the creek in the same place he had crossed before.

He knelt down and looked around as he tried to think. Where could the patrol have gone? He had not heard any shooting, nor had he heard any noise from the men or their horses.

He thought about calling out, but knew if anyone was around he would give away their position. Letting someone know their position could prove fatal for all of them.

If the patrol was not here, then the men must have withdrawn back to where Johnson was holding the horses. Maybe the sergeant had decided to pull back away from the creek to get closer to the horses in case they were needed in a hurry.

The other possibility was they had moved somewhere along the creek to find better cover. He decided if he put the creek on his left and started down stream, he should find the patrol.

Corporal Hayes slowly began working his way further away from the creek. He kept low to the ground in an effort to see any tracks left by the patrol. He hadn't gone far when he noticed a dark wet spot on the trail.

He took a minute to look around before he knelt down next to the dark spot. He removed his glove and touched the dark spot with the tips of his fingers. When he got his fingers closer to his face where he could see it better, he could see it was dark red and sticky. He quickly realized that it was blood. A chill went through him as he looked around, but he could only see but a few yards in any direction.

Corporal Hayes looked again at the blood on his fingers. He moved away from the bloody spot on the ground and ducked down next to a fallen tree. He leaned up against the tree and let out a long sigh, then closed his eyes and listened very carefully for some sound, any sound that would give him some idea of what was going on. He heard nothing, not even the sound of a bird.

As Corporal Hayes sat next to the tree, he began to think. He couldn't believe he had been left behind. He knew Sergeant Wells would never leave a man behind if he could help it.

It occurred to Corporal Hayes that something must have happened to make them leave him behind. The blood on the ground was an indication that whatever it was, it had been quick and violent. There had been no gunshots, no screams, no nothing. Yet, there had to be an explanation why he had been left.

Looking at the ground while he was thinking, he saw marks in the dirt. They were the same kind of marks that might be made by a man's boots if he had been dragged.

Moving very carefully, Corporal Hayes began following the marks. He had not gone more than a few feet when he discovered a pair of boots behind a large log. The boots were the kind of boots worn by a cavalryman.

Slowly, he moved around so he could see behind the log. There on the ground laid the men from the patrol. They were all laid out very neatly and their throats had been cut.

The unexpected sight of the dead cavalrymen caused Corporal Hayes to quickly duck back down behind the fallen tree and gasp for air. He had seen a lot of death during the war, but this was different. Each and every one of them had been killed without a chance to fight back.

Corporal Hayes knew it was not safe for him there. He had to move to a safer place. But before he could leave, he should make sure all the men were dead. If there was even one of them still alive, he had to find him. If they were all dead, he should try to get back to the fort and report what had happened as soon as possible.

Corporal Hayes swallowed hard, took a deep breath and then looked back at the bodies of the dead soldiers. They were all there except for Private Johnson and Sergeant Wells. He quickly turned around and sat back down.

Johnson was the only one of the patrol that had been left behind to tend the horses. Sergeant Wells had been with the others when he crossed the creek to investigate the sounds.

Where were Johnson and Wells now? Corporal Hayes remembered they had left the horses further down the trail. If he could find where they were held he might be able to find Private Johnson.

Another look at the ground surrounding the dead soldiers produced another set of tracks. They had not been made by cavalry boots or by Indian moccasins. They had been made by boots, white man's boots. This caused Hayes to think it may have been white men that raided the wagon train. He was certain that it had been white men who had murdered the members of the patrol.

Corporal Hayes started to move toward where the horses had been left. When he got to the place where Johnson should have been, the horses were gone. However, he did find Private Johnson. Like the other cavalrymen, his throat had been cut.

There was only one member of the patrol not accounted for. What had happened to Sergeant Wells? Had he been taken prisoner? That hardly seemed likely since all the rest had been murdered. Had he been killed somewhere else? Was it possible he had escaped?

At this point, Corporal Hayes wasn't sure what he should do. The longer he stayed in the area, the more likely it was that he would be found. On the other hand, he couldn't sneak off without knowing what had happened to the sergeant.

He sat down next to a big cottonwood tree and listened, but he heard nothing. Then he heard a bird in a nearby tree. If a bird was singing it was unlikely anyone was close by.

Corporal Hayes thought about what he should do. The fort was about five days away on foot. If he left without knowing what had happened to Sergeant Wells, others at the fort might look at him as a soldier who would desert one of his fellow men. If he stayed around and looked for Wells, he might not get back to the fort at all to tell them what happened.

It didn't seem to matter what he decided. The more he thought about it, the more he began to accept the fact that Sergeant Wells would not leave him, so he would not leave without knowing what happened to the sergeant.

Corporal Hayes took in a deep breath as he looked up. He could see the fog was lifting a little. At this point, there was nothing else for him to do but to go back to the campsite and see if the man in the bedroll was still alive.

Corporal Hayes worked his way back toward the campsite. It had started to snow. This was both good and bad. It was good from the standpoint that he would be able to see any fresh tracks. From the tracks he would be able to find out if any of the raiders were still around and which way they went.

It was bad from the standpoint that he would be leaving tracks wherever he went. That meant they could follow him. He doubted they would want to leave any witnesses.

When he came near the clearing where the campsite was, the fire was still smoldering. There were no more yellow flames dancing on the logs. The snow was beginning to stick to the ground.

He carefully examined the ground in the clearing. There were no tracks in the fresh snow. He looked behind him at his own tracks. The thick heavy snow was quickly covering them. In a matter of minutes his tracks would no longer exist.

He turned his attention to the bedroll. There was no movement and no sounds. Corporal Hayes was beginning to think the man in the bedroll was dead. There was only one way to find out.

Corporal Hayes looked around again. He could barely see across the clearing as the snow was falling hard. He didn't see anyone. He leaned his rifle up against a tree and drew his pistol from his holster. Half crouched down, he started into the clearing. He moved close to the bedroll. Taking one last look around, he reached out and pulled the covers off the man's face.

The man didn't move, nor did he open his eyes. At first Corporal Hayes thought he was dead, but the slight signs of breathing assured him that the man was still alive.

Corporal Hayes reached out and touched the man's shoulder. Slowly the man opened his eyes and looked up. There was no emotion in the man's eyes, only the look of pain on his face. There was no fear in his eyes, nothing except for acceptance of the fact that he was going to die.

Corporal Hayes lifted up the bedroll so he could see how badly the man was injured. He discovered the man had been gut shot, a slow and painful way to die.

"Help - - me," the man whispered so softly Corporal Hayes could hardly hear him.

"There's nothing I can do for you."

"Shoot - - - me. Please," the man begged.

Corporal Hayes knew if it were him, he would hope someone would kill him to stop the pain. The corporal thought about it, but he needed the man alive for a little while longer. He knew the man was a hard man and it would not be easy to get out of him what he needed to know.

"Not until you tell me where your friends were headed."

The man looked up at him. The corporal was not sure if he had succeeded in making his request clear.

"Where were you going?"

"They - - are headed - - for - - Deadwood," the man said after looking into the corporal's face for a minute or two.

"What are they going to do there?"

"They - - are going - - to take - - the supplies - - from the - - wagon train - - to Deadwood - - to sell - - to the miners," the man said his voice showing the pain he was in.

"How are they going to do that?"

"They - - will take - - them to - - MacFee, Jason MacFee."

Corporal Hayes had been through Deadwood a time or two. He knew Jason MacFee ran the General Store in Deadwood. Pretty neat plan, he thought. Steal from the wagon trains and sell the supplies through a general store. That made it all profit without having to deal with others.

Corporal Hayes stood up and looked off toward the west. He couldn't see anything as it was still snowing very hard. He was thinking. He wondered who the leader was. Was it MacFee, or was it someone else?

"Shoot - - me. Please," the man begged again.

The plea from the man caused Corporal Hayes to look back down at him. He was not going to shoot him. The man was part of a gang that had killed the rest of his patrol. The man had chosen a life of crime. Now he would die a slow painful death because of the path in life he had chosen to take. Besides, a gunshot might give the corporal's position away.

Corporal Hayes simply stood up, turned and walked back to where he had left his rifle. As far as he knew, he was the only one left in his patrol. He knew the information he had was important, too important for him to risk his life by going after the killers of his patrol, or take up valuable time looking for Sergeant Wells. He had to get the information back to the fort as quickly as possible.

Corporal Hayes crossed back over the creek and headed north toward Fort Meade. Fort Meade had a pretty good sized garrison.

The snow began to lighten up some making it easier to see. It also seemed to be warming up, which caused the snow to melt quickly.

He hadn't gone far when he saw what looked like a blue jacket or coat on the ground. He crouched down and began working his way toward the coat. He was only a few yards from the coat when he realized it was Sergeant Wells. He jumped up, ran to him.

"Sergeant," Corporal Hayes called out as he dropped down beside him.

"Good to see you," the sergeant said, the sound of pain in his voice.

"What happened?" Corporal Hayes asked as he started to open the sergeant's coat and check his wound.

Corporal Hayes found a nasty looking wound to the sergeant's shoulder. He immediately started to make a dressing for it in an effort to stop the bleeding.

While Corporal Hayes dressed Sergeant Wells' wound, the sergeant explained what had happened.

The gang that had robbed the wagon train of its supplies had attacked them. It had been done with such speed they never knew what hit them. The one who had attacked Sergeant Wells had almost succeeded in killing him, but the raider's knife had missed any vital organs. It had gone in under the sergeant's collarbone next to his shoulder. The young raider was scared and had thought he had killed him. Sergeant Wells had crawled off and hid in a thicket until the raiders gave up looking for him, then moved on. He had lost a lot of blood and was weak, but alive.

"I didn't dare call out to you. If I had they would have found both of us," Sergeant Wells said.

"I'm glad you stayed quiet. I was able to find out what was going on."

Corporal Hayes explained what he had found out about the robbery of the wagon train and where they were taking the supplies. He also explained he was going to Fort Meade to report what he found out.

"You have to get there as fast as you can," Sergeant Wells said.

"I can't leave you here," Corporal Hayes insisted.

"You have to. If they get the supplies to MacFee, the major will never catch the thieves."

"Yes, they will. MacFee is the leader."

"But you can't prove it," Sergeant Wells insisted.

"I can. A search of his store goods will show they were stolen from the Army supply train."

"You better get going. I'll be all right here until you get back."

"No. It's getting too cold. You'll freeze to death when night comes."

The sergeant looked at the corporal's face. It was clear there was no use in arguing with him.

"Okay," Sergeant Wells agreed reluctantly.

It would be less than an hour before it would start getting dark. The air was cold and a fire would be needed if they were going to get through the night without freezing. The only things they had were the coats they were wearing to keep warm. To build a fire meant if the men who had raided the wagon train were still around, it might be seen. They would have to find a ravine or draw where they could build a small fire.

Corporal Hayes helped Sergeant Wells to his feet and started off toward the north. They walked at a slow, yet steady pace. It was one that would conserve energy, yet still make progress toward the fort.

As night was coming upon them, they found a deep ravine. It wandered up into the hills to the west and meandered out onto the prairie to the east.

"This looks like a good place to settle in for the night," Corporal Hayes suggested.

"Okay," Sergeant Wells agreed.

It was clear that the sergeant was tired. Hayes was sure he would not be able to go on much longer without some rest.

Once they were down inside the ravine, Hayes found a place where he hoped it would be easy to hide a small fire. They settled in until they heard a voice.

"I'll bet you boys in blue thought you got away. Well, you didn't."

Sergeant Wells looked at Corporal Hayes. They then looked both ways down the ravine, but couldn't see anyone.

"We can't let them catch us," Sergeant Wells whispered. "If they do, there will be no one to tell Major Westby what happened to the patrol or who robbed the wagon train. I'll hold them off while you get away."

"I can't leave you here to fight them off. There's too many of them."

"I doubt all of them are here. They'll want to get the supplies to Deadwood as soon as possible. They won't want to risk not getting them there. Besides, I'm in no condition to travel."

Corporal Hayes knew he was right. The chances of both of them escaping were pretty slim. One of them might have a chance if the other could keep the raiders busy. There was little else they could do if they were to get word to the fort.

"Okay. There's a cut off to another ravine down that way. If I can get to it, I might be able to escape."

"Good. You best get going. It'll be dark shortly. You have to get far enough away so they can't find you. Good luck," Sergeant Wells said as he stuck out his hand.

Corporal Hayes looked at his hand for a second and then reached out and took it.

"You're a good soldier, Sergeant," Corporal Hayes said, then quickly turned and started down the ravine.

He didn't bother to turn and look back. Corporal Hayes had a job to do. If he could get word to the fort, these raiders might be stopped before another wagon train was robbed or another patrol was massacred.

As Corporal Hayes got to the place were the other ravine joined up with the one he was in, he heard gunshots being fired. He hesitated only a second. He thought about running back to help the sergeant, but that was not what he had to do.

Just as he turned the corner to go up the other ravine, he ran into one of the raiders. It was such a surprise to both of them that Hayes simply ran into the man and knocked him to the ground.

Corporal Hayes began hitting the man in the face with the barrel of his pistol, again and again, until the man didn't move any more. Out of breath, he sat on top of the man and looked down at his bloody face. He turned and looked back toward where he had come from. It was quiet now. There were no more sounds of gunfire. He knew it was over for Sergeant Wells.

Just then, the man below Corporal Hayes moaned. It was a soft moan, but a sound the corporal could not afford to have anyone hear. He put his hand over the raider's mouth while he pulled a knife from his belt. He held the knife at the man's throat. The raider opened his eyes and looked up at Hayes.

"Is this how you killed my men?" Corporal Hayes asked, then he pushed the knife down hard cutting his throat.

The man squirmed a little, then went limp. He was dead.

Corporal Hayes looked at him for only a few seconds before he got up and began running along the ravine. He knew he had to put as much distance as he could between him and the raiders.

It was four days later when Corporal Hayes stumbled into Fort Meade tired and hungry. He was quickly taken to Major Westby where he reported what had happened to the wagon train, its supplies and to the patrol.

The major quickly formed a company to go after the raiders and MacFee in Deadwood. He gave orders to Corporal Hayes to get some food and some rest. In the morning, he was to get a patrol together to go back to where Sergeant Wells' body could be found and retrieve it. He was also to retrieve the bodies of the rest of the patrol and return them to the fort for a proper military burial.

# THE SHOOT-OUT

It was a cold winter night in 1888 when a man walked into the Golden Nugget Saloon in the mining town of Lead in the Dakota Territory. He wore a long black frock coat and a black hat with a silver hatband. As he stepped into the saloon, he stopped at the door and brushed the snow off his coat and shook the snow off his hat. He looked around the room and found everyone in the room watching him.

"Howdy, folks."

No one responded to the man's comment other than to simply nod. The man took off his gloves and his coat, and laid them over a chair at an empty table. He then laid his hat on the table.

The stranger was dressed like a gambler with a hint of gunfighter mixed in. He wore a long sleeved white shirt under a fitted waist jacket and a black string tie. His nickel-plated six-shooter with Mother of Pearl handgrips hung low on his hip and was tied down on his leg. His trousers were well tailored and tucked inside his boots. The boots he wore were black with shiny silver spurs and a small knife was tucked inside the top of his left boot. Everything about the man made a person want to take notice of him.

"Sure enough is cold out there," he said with a big grin as he walked toward the bar while rubbing his hands together in an effort to warm them.

"What'll it be, mister?" the barkeeper asked.

"A hot cup of coffee to warm my hands and a good shot of whiskey to warm my insides," the man said as he casually glanced toward the two men leaning up against the bar.

The barkeeper set a coffee cup and a shot glass on the bar, then walked over to a potbelly stove and picked up a coffee pot. He returned to the bar where he filled both the cup and the shot glass.

The stranger picked up the whiskey and tossed it down, then set the glass back on the bar. He took hold of the cup of coffee, wrapped his fingers around it and held it in both hands. It was a long time before he took a sip of the hot liquid.

The man turned around and leaned back against the bar. He stood there looking around the room. It was not a very busy night. Only seven people were in the bar, eight counting himself. There was the barkeeper behind the bar and a saloon girl at a table in the corner talking with a young cowboy. Two men were playing a card game. They seemed more interested in talking than in playing since there was no money on the table.

Then there were two men standing at the bar. They looked like cowboys. One looked like he might have experienced a bit more of the world than the other.

The man immediately noticed how one of them at the bar wore his gun, and that he had red clay on his boots. The other didn't have the red clay on his boots causing him to think they had not been riding together very long.

"My name is Wilfred Horner. My friends call me Will. I came here to relax and maybe play a friendly game of poker."

"You a gunfighter?" one of the men at the bar asked.

Will turned and looked the man over. He studied him a bit, then smiled. The question had come from the cowboy with the red clay on his boots.

"What might they call you, friend?" Will ask politely.

"First of all, I ain't your friend. Secondly, I asked you a question. When I ask a man a question, I expect an answer."

"I was just interested in finding out who you are. I didn't mean to ruffle your tail feathers none," Will said, his voice showing a slight tone of apology.

The young man straightened up as he set his drink down on the bar. He planted his feet as if he were looking for a fight. Will took note and kept eye contact with the man. The fact he had a cup of coffee in his hands did not reduce Will's readiness if the young man wanted to push it.

"Now I don't know what your problem is, but I came in here to warm up, have a drink and play a little cards. I'm sure these fine folks here would rather not see a gunfight. Someone could get hurt. We don't want that, do we?" Will asked as he casually set his cup on the bar.

The young man took a minute to look over Will and began to wonder if maybe he had pressed his luck a little. He was beginning to think the stranger might really be a gunfighter.

"Mr. Horner, I don't think my friend meant anything by it," the other man at the bar said, the tone of his voice showing he was worried about how this might turn out.

"You good friends?" Will asked.

"Yeah, I'd like to think so."

"In that case, I think you should teach your friend some manners. When a person introduces himself, the proper thing to do is to say, "Howdy," and then introduce yourself. Don't you think?"

"Yes, sir. I surely do agree with you on that. My name is Billy Smith, and this here is my friend Walt Barrells."

"Nice to meet you, Mr. Smith, and your friend Walt Barrells."

Will watched as Billy reached out and touched Walt on the shoulder. Walt hesitated for a moment before he turned his head and looked at Billy. He then turned back around toward the bar. It was over, at least for the moment. The last thing Will wanted was to get into a gunfight with some kid who thought he could make himself a reputation by killing a gunfighter.

Will turned back toward the bar and picked up his cup of coffee. He kept an eye on the mirror behind the bar to make sure Walt was not going to do anything stupid. He had seen young men like Walt before. They had such a need to make a reputation for themselves that they would risk their own life to get one. The few that had succeeded usually ended up dead before they reached their twenty-fifth birthday. The one thing they never seemed to understand was when you have a reputation as a gunfighter, there's always someone who wants to get his reputation by gunning you down. It becomes a vicious circle. The proof was in the fact there were very few old gunfighters.

"Barkeep, can a man get something to eat around here?"

"Sure. I can rustle you up a steak and a few potatoes if that's good enough?"

"That would be fine. Mind if I refill this cup?"

"Not at all. Help yourself."

Will took his cup over to the potbelly stove and filled it. As he did he kept an eye on the kid. Deep down he knew the kid was going to drink up enough courage to take him on in a gunfight. It was something he had seen time and time again.

Will walked across the room to a table in the corner and sat down with his back to the wall. He spent the time he had waiting for his dinner watching the others in the room, especially Walt. Every once in a while, Walt would look over his shoulder at Will. It made Will feel a little uneasy.

When Will's dinner came, he pulled himself up to the table to eat. He took his time and enjoyed the meal. He had learned a long time ago that every meal could be your last.

The more Will watched the young man, the more he began to believe that he was the man he had been hunting. He didn't have a very good description of the man he wanted, but the young man was close.

Will had no more than finished his meal when the saloon girl came over to his table and sat down across the table from him. She was wearing a dress much like those worn by the dance hall girls in Kansas City, but this small saloon was nothing like the fancy dance halls in Kansas City.

Will had to admit she was a good-looking young woman even if she did use a little too much rouge. Her eyes seemed to sparkle and were as blue as the afternoon sky. Her long blond curls hung down onto her bare shoulder.

"Need a little company, mister?"

"I never refuse the company of a lovely young lady, but what about your friend over there?"

She quickly glanced at the young man she had been sitting with in the corner. He was upset with her for leaving him.

"He knows a girl's gotta make a living."

Will looked over at the young man in the corner again. He had seen young men like him before, too. Will could tell the young man was working up the nerve to challenge him for the girl.

"What's your name?" he asked.

"Mary Bell."

"Well, Mary Bell, that's a very pretty name."

"Do you want me to keep you company or not?"

"Get us a drink," he said softly.

Mary Bell looked at him for a minute and then smiled. She turned and walked over to the bar. The barkeeper poured two whiskeys, she picked them up and returned to the table.

As she approached the table, Will once again glanced over at the young man in the corner. Will had no desire to get into it with him.

"Why don't you take those drinks and go over there with your boyfriend. I'm sure you would rather be with him anyway."

She looked surprised. She couldn't believe what he was telling her to do. She looked over at her boyfriend.

"I saw the way you look at him. You're in love with him. Do yourself, and him, a big favor and get out of here. You don't belong in a place like this," Will said as he looked up at her.

Mary Bell was not sure what to do. She had never met a man like him before.

"Get out of here and take your boyfriend with you. Get married, build yourselves a home and raise a lot of kids," he said with a smile.

A smile slowly came over her face as she began to understand what it was he was saying. She did love the young man and wanted more than anything to be with him.

"Thank you, mister," she said with a smile.

Will nodded, then watched her as she walked across the room toward the young man. He was feeling a bit pleased with himself, but it was to be short lived.

"Hey! You, girl. Get over here," Walt called.

Mary Bell stopped, looked at Walt, then turned and looked at Will. She wasn't sure what she should do.

"Let her go," Will said softly, but with a strong tone of authority in his voice.

"No. She's here to keep us company on these cold lonely nights," Walt said, the tone of his voice daring anyone to interfere.

"You don't have to do anything you don't want to do," Will said to Mary Bell.

"You mind your own business," Walt said sharply.

Will was very much aware of what was going on in Walt's head. He knew Walt had no interest in Mary Bell. Walt wanted a fight with Will, and Will knew there was no way out of it. It had been inevitable from the moment he walked in the door of the dreary saloon.

"You don't care about her. Let her go to her boyfriend," Will said calmly.

Walt had been drinking pretty steady since Will had arrived. Will had no idea how long he had been drinking before he got there, but it didn't matter. The kid was looking for a fight. Will had provided him with a challenge that could make him a big man in the eyes of some.

What Walt did not know was he had no idea who he was challenging. Walt was sure Will was a gunfighter. What he didn't know was that Will was one of the best. Will was not well known except in the southwest Arizona Territory.

The kid also didn't know Will was one of the best bounty hunters in the west. It was not by accident that Will Horner was in Lead. He was here to take a killer back to Yuma to stand trial for the murder of a state prison guard.

"Maybe I'll just shoot her boyfriend," Walt threatened as he glanced over at the young man sitting at the table.

While he was looking toward the young man, Will carefully slipped his gun out of his holster and held it in his lap.

"I wouldn't try that if I were you," Will said calmly.

"And why not?"

"Walt, take a good look at him," Billy said quietly so only Walt could hear him. "His hand's under the table."

Walt's hand had been slowly moving closer to his gun. As soon as his eyes went to the table, he pulled his hand away. Walt's eyes got big. The expression on his face showed he was angry that a tinhorn gambler had the drop on him.

"Go to your boyfriend and the two of you get out of here," Will said to Mary Bell, never once taking his eyes off Walt.

She hesitated only a second before she quickly moved across the room. She set the drinks on the table and reached out a hand to the cowboy.

"Come on, Bobby," she said as she pulled him out of the chair.

Will could see the anger grow in Walt's eyes as he watched Bobby and Mary Bell leave out the back of the saloon. As soon as they were gone, Walt turned back and looked at Will.

"You're going to be sorry you did that."

"I doubt it."

"Let it go, Walt. You've had too much to drink. Let's go," Billy said as he reached out and touched Walt's shoulder.

The kid shrugged his shoulder and moved away from Billy. He looked at Billy with scorn. Billy couldn't understand Walt's actions. All he seemed to know was that Walt was determined to get into a shoot-out.

"I'm leaving. I don't want any trouble. I'm going back to the ranch. Are you coming or not?"

"No," Walt said sharply.

"Suit yourself. I'm dealing myself out of this."

"You go back to the ranch. I'll be along as soon as I take care of business here."

Billy shook his head and started toward the door. He was smart not to want to get involved in a shoot-out with a man like Will Horner. He didn't like the idea of leaving his friend to face a gunfighter alone, but if Walt wanted to be stupid there was nothing he could do about it.

Billy had had the chance to see the results of a gunfight with a gunslinger before. It was not a pretty sight. Even though he knew Walt was fast with a gun, he had a gut feeling that Will Horner was a professional and probably faster than Walt.

Billy stopped at the door. Before he pushed it open, he looked back at Walt in the hope he would come. When he didn't, Billy turned and walked out of the saloon. The only people in the saloon now were Will, the barkeeper and Walt.

The two card players had quietly ducked out at the first sign of trouble. They knew men like Walt didn't care who they killed.

"If you guys are going to go at it, you can take it outside. I don't want no gunfightin' in here," the barkeeper said.

"I don't think it will be necessary," Will said, his voice showing no emotion as he continued to watch the kid.

"No, I like it here just fine."

Walt had a self-assured stupid grin on his face. He had no idea what he had gotten himself into, much less how to get out of it. His drinking had been doing his talking for him and had talked him into something that was way over his head.

Will wanted no surprises from the kid. Besides, he had no idea how good a gunfighter Walt might be. Like all of the gunfights Will had been in, he would go at it as if his life depended on it, because it did.

"Let's get down to what this is really about," Will said calmly.

"Yeah, that's a good idea. What is this really about? You seem to know me, but I don't know you. I like to know who I kill," Walt said with a slight snicker.

Walt felt that he was finally going to get his way. This tinhorn gambler was going to make him well known as a gunfighter.

"First of all, I happen to know you are not Walt Barrells. Your real name is John Small, or as your friends liked to call you, Johnny Small," Will said.

Will noticed the look on Johnny's face when he said his real name. It was clear Johnny was suddenly paying more attention.

"You and your friends robbed a bank in Yuma, Arizona, and got caught. You were tried and sentenced to serve ten years in the state prison. You served only two years when you and three others tried to escape. Any of this ring a bell with you?"

Will continued to watch Johnny's face. He didn't respond to Will's question. He could tell by the change in Johnny's expression that he had the right man. When Johnny didn't say anything, Will continued, his hand still on the gun that he held in his lap under the table.

"Your friends were killed in their attempt to escape, but you got away. You came up here to hide on a ranch as a ranch hand.

Someone from here was in Yuma and saw your wanted poster. He told me about you."

"You're a bounty hunter," Johnny said with surprise.

"That's right," Will replied.

"You came all the way up here to take me back to prison?"

"In your case, you're worth the trouble."

"How much is it worth to you to take me back?"

"One thousand dollars," Will replied.

"A thousand dollars! That's a lot of money."

"Yes, it is. The state of Arizona wants you back. You killed one of their prison guards. They want to make an example out of you."

"Well, I hate to disappoint them, but I ain't goin' back."

"You're not?"

"No, I'm not."

"By the way, did I mention the poster said they wanted you dead or alive? I don't think they really care which. Either way they get what they want, and I get paid."

Johnny was watching Will very carefully. He knew Will had a gun in his lap, but he was still wondering if he could beat him to the draw. He kept running it through his mind that he was fast, but he hadn't quite convinced himself that he was fast enough to beat the bounty hunter when he already had a gun in his hand. He was itching to try. Even with the whiskey telling him how good he was, he didn't have the nerve.

All Johnny could think of was how could he get this guy to put his gun in his holster so they could have a fair fight. He was sure he could beat him in a fair fight.

"Do you think you could get me back to Yuma alive? I don't think you can. I don't even think you will be able to get me out of this saloon," Johnny said with a smirk.

"You're bound and determined to get yourself killed, aren't you, kid?"

"No. I ain't goin' back to jail. I know you got a gun in your hand. The minute you try to stand up and pull that gun out from under that table, I'm goin'a kill you," he said with a note of confidence.

Will took a second or two to think about what he had said, never once taking his eyes off Johnny or changing the expression on his face. He knew he was not in the best position for a fight. His back was too close to the wall. He lacked the room he needed to maneuver his gun quickly, and he was sure this young man was quick. He couldn't believe he had put himself in such a position.

"So what do we do? I'm not going to let you walk out of here. I've spent too much time finding you," Will said, patiently waiting for Johnny to make a mistake.

"I'm here at the bar. I've got the barkeeper to bring me whatever I want, so I've got all night," Johnny said with a slight laugh.

"So you do, but I've already got my gun pointed at your gut. All I have to do is pull the trigger. Have you ever seen a man die of a gunshot wound to the gut?" Will asked.

Johnny's eyes began to get big as it began to seep into his whiskey soaked brain that he could be killed. It suddenly occurred to him this might not work out. The bounty hunter could pull the trigger any time he wanted and there would be no warning, none at all. He could not see Will's trigger finger so he would never know when it was coming.

"Well, what's it going to be?" Will asked, showing a little impatience with him.

Johnny kept looking at Will. He was beginning to understand this was not working out at all. It was either give up to him or draw. Either way, it was going to mean the end of his life.

Will knew what choices Johnny had and there were few. He patiently waited for Johnny to decide what he was going to do. He could see Johnny was turning over the choices he had in his head. Will had no allusions of what might happen. Johnny was cornered, and like a cornered animal he might do anything. He was hoping Johnny would not act too quickly. If the liquor had a chance to wear off a little, he might see that it was over and give up.

Johnny tipped his head down slightly and looked at the floor in front of him. He was thinking about what he should do. After a minute or so, he slowly lifted his head up.

Will had seen that look in other men's eyes before. It was the look of a person who had made a decision and he was going to play out the cards dealt to him no matter what the outcome. Johnny soon convinced himself that there was no option to fold.

"Don't do anything stupid, Johnny," Will warned him, but he knew it was too late.

Johnny slowly shrugged his shoulder and planted his feet firmly on the floor. He looked at Will for a few seconds, then grabbed for his gun. The room filled with the sounds of gunshots and the smell of gunpowder.

The bullet from Will's gun struck Johnny in the stomach just an inch above his belt buckle. It pushed him back against the bar and caused him to slump forward and fall on the floor.

Johnny's gun was still in his hand. He had almost cleared leather when the bullet from Will's gun ripped into him. The impact of the bullet had caused Johnny to pull the trigger on his gun, but his bullet went through the saloon floor a foot in front of him.

Will pushed back from the table and got up. He walked across the room toward Johnny. He knelt down, took the gun from the kid's hand and tossed it across the room. Turning Johnny over, he saw the large bloody spot on the front of his shirt. He looked at Johnny's face.

"I told you not to try it," Will said, his voice showing he was angry.

"Yeah," Johnny replied weakly. "But I told - - - you that I - - - wouldn't go back - - - to prison," he said, growing weaker with each passing second.

"Yes, you did," Will admitted, as he watched Johnny take his last breath.

It was only a few minutes before the barkeeper got a couple of men to take Johnny's body out back to the icehouse where he would remain until he was buried in the morning. Will sat down and had another drink. It was over. He had done his job. Tomorrow he would head back to Yuma and collect his money.

# A DIARY FROM THE PLAINS

Joshua Weatherby, a former trapper, Army scout, and Wagon Master, was riding his horse and leading a pack horse west along the Oregon Trail. The smell of rain began to fill the air. He looked up at the sky and immediately knew he should find a place to take shelter. He moved off the open ground and down into the large cottonwood trees that grew along the banks of the Platte River. He immediately began looking for a place where he could build a shelter.

Joshua reined up at the unexpected sight of a Conestoga wagon in among the trees near the river. He stared at the large broad-wheeled wagon as if he was looking at a ghost. He had not seen anyone for days, but to see a wagon so close to the river was surprising to say the least.

Most of the Oregon Trail was away from the river. The trees, sandy soil along the banks of the river and the many ravines and gullies made travel close to the river almost impossible. The wagons were not as likely to get bogged down if they stayed where the ground was solid and open. In some places the trail was over two miles from the river to make travel easier for both man and beast.

Joshua looked around to see if anyone was near by. The first things he looked for were the oxen it would take to move such a heavy wagon. There were no oxen, no mules and no horses anywhere in sight. In fact, there were no signs of life at all.

Curious as to what the wagon was doing there, he nudged his horses closer. When he was still a hundred feet or so away from the wagon, he reined up again. He swung his leg over the saddle and stepped down from his horse.

Keeping one eye on the wagon, he tied his horses to a cottonwood tree and removed his rifle from his saddle scabbard. He levered a round into the chamber and began moving closer to the wagon.

Joshua moved carefully toward the wagon. The last thing he wanted was to be caught in a trap, even though he had nothing of value but his horses.

As he moved closer, he looked for something that would explain why the wagon was there. There were no tracks to tell him where it had come from, and no hint of where it was going. The fact it was in among the trees caused him to wonder why anyone would bring such a heavy wagon down along the riverbank. He could see that it had sunk almost a foot into the soft sandy soil.

The closer Joshua got to the wagon, the more he began to realize that it had been there for some time. The canvas top was dirty and there were weeds growing up and around the wheels. The tongue of the wagon was gone and the harnesses were badly weathered from being left uncared for on the ground.

As Joshua approached the wagon, he noticed three crosses in a row about twenty feet from the wagon. The sand was mounded up in front of the crosses indicating that three people had been buried there. He stood quietly looking at the graves and wondering who had been buried there.

There was a sudden flash of lightning followed by the loud crash of thunder. He looked up in time to feel the first few drops of rain.

The only place of shelter was either inside the wagon or under it. Joshua ran to his horses and untied them. He led them over next to the wagon and tied them to one of the wheels. He removed the packs from his packhorses and stuffed them under the wagon. He removed his saddle and put it under the tarp he used to cover his supplies.

He decided he might stay drier if he were inside the wagon. It occurred to him there might be something in the wagon that would help him to figure out why the wagon was there.

Joshua jumped into the wagon as the rain became a downpour. He looked up and listened as the rain pelted the canvas top. He wasn't sure the canvas would hold up, but soon realized that it was still in good condition. The fact that the canvas top was in good shape meant the wagon might not have been there as long as he thought, maybe two or three months at the most.

He sat down and leaned back against the sideboards and looked around. There were two large trunks that had been left in the wagon. Although things were covered with dirt, they were dry and in good shape. He figured the canvas top had kept things dry.

Joshua was hesitant to open the trunks because they were someone's private property. He began to reason that if he wanted to know who the wagon belonged to and who was in the graves, he would have to look in the trunks.

Opening the first trunk he found mostly clothes, blankets and quilts. The clothes indicated the wagon belonged to a family. He pawed through the entire trunk, but found nothing that would help him in his quest for information.

The second trunk contained some bedding, a few pots and pans, and some small tools and hardware supplies. It also contained sheets of paper and a few books, including a Bible. The books were mostly books used to learn arithmetic, spelling, and reading. Whoever the wagon belonged to, they had planned to educate their children.

He found one other book, a diary. Joshua thought if he read the diary, he might find out what had happened. He carefully, almost reverently, opened the diary. He fanned through the diary, stopping near the last few pages that had writing on them and began to read it.

*June 24ᵗʰ, 1856. Dear Diary, Today the sun was shining and the sky was such a bright blue it almost hurt my eyes to look at it. The tall green grasses of the prairie waved in the gentle breeze like waves in the ocean back in Virginia on a calm summer evening, only green instead of blue. Today marks two months of travel. The going has been slow, but we are making progress toward our new home in the Promised Land. Today I saw a herd of Antelope on a hillside. Several of the men went out to hunt them, but the animals moved off well out of range. They are a shy animal and look so beautiful. I wish we did not have to hunt them. I am glad the men were more successful hunting deer. We now have some fresh meat to eat. It has been a long day and I am tired. I will say goodnight, Diary. Jenny.*

Joshua looked at the handwriting and wondered how old the person was who had written it. He felt as if she might be young because she seemed to see things with the eyes of the young and hopeful. Even after months of hard travel across the prairie she was still optimistic.

Joshua wanted to know more about the woman or young girl who could see things like she did. He turned the page and began to read the next entry in the diary.

*June 25th 1856. Dear Diary, Today it rained and several of the wagons got stuck in the mud. We did not make very much progress toward our goal. It took everyone to keep the wagons moving. There is a breeze this evening and Mr. Moffett thinks if it does not rain again, we should be able to make better progress tomorrow. Some of our belongings got a little damp due to the sudden storm, but nothing was lost. The small children have been collecting buffalo droppings to put in the nets hung under the wagons. The droppings are used for fires for cooking. There are very few trees to get wood from except along the edge of the river. We only get close to the river every few days. Sometimes we have to walk almost a mile to get water. Mr. Moffett says if we get too close to the river, the wagons will get bogged down in the sandy soil. I guess he knows what he is talking about as he has been over this trail many times. I spent part of the day helping with the care of the small children. Again, it is late and it has been a long day. I have written this by the light of the fire. Goodnight, Diary. Jenny.*

The last part of the diary gave Joshua a little more insight into the writer of the diary. He felt she might be a girl in her late teens as she had helped with the children. There was no indication that any of the children were hers.

Mr. Moffett was obviously the Wagon Master on the trip west. Wanting to know more, he read the entry for the next day.

*June 26th 1856. Dear Diary, Today we saw several Indians up on a ridge only a little ways away from us. They sat on their ponies and watched as the wagon train slowly moved across the vast, almost endless, prairie. One of the men said they were a hunting party and they meant us no harm. I took notice of one of them. He came down off the hill and rode fairly close to the wagons to look at us. I think he was as interested in us as we were in him. He was a young brave and sat on a pony that looked strong and fast. He had a single feather in his long black hair and carried a long lance with several feathers on it. There was a single feather in the mane of his pony as well. He sat his pony very straight and looked rather noble, I thought, for a savage. His skin was dark brown with a reddish tinge to it, which I'm sure is why they call them "red men". I found it strange that he wore very little in the way of clothes. Mother did not want me looking at him, but I could not help it. I thought he was a beautiful looking man, but I am sure mother would not see it that way. It is late and I must get some rest so I will say goodnight. Goodnight, Diary. Jenny.*

Joshua was getting a little embarrassed at reading about the woman's most personal thoughts. He hesitated to read any further, but he still needed to know what had happened. Joshua skipped a couple of pages and began reading again.

*June 29th 1856. Dear Diary, Today two members of the McCollin family took ill. Mr. Moffett said it was best if we separated ourselves from them. Mr. McCollin did not like it when Mr. Moffett and several of the other men in the wagon train made Mr. McCollin move his wagon away from the rest of us. They had to move to the rear of the wagon train. When we stopped for the night, they had to camp away from the rest of the wagons. I heard some of the men talking about it. They were afraid the McCollins had come down with Cholera. I heard Mr. Moffett tell a couple of the men that they were to stand guard and make sure none of the McCollins came into camp. I am a little scared, as I had found the McCollins to be very nice people. I do not understand what is happening. I have heard it said they might die and any of us could get sick from them. Father instructed us to make sure we stayed away from the McCollins until we are absolutely sure they do not have Cholera. I doubt I will sleep very well tonight. Goodnight, Diary. Jenny.*

Joshua looked out the back of the wagon. He wasn't looking at anything in particular, but rather staring off into space. If what Jenny was saying was true, the wagon he was sitting in could be a wagon whose members got Cholera and died. The only other thing he had learned from the diary was there were several members to this family, Jenny, her father, her mother and one or more smaller children.

Joshua looked back at the diary as he thought about the three graves. He had to wonder if it had been Cholera that had taken the three who were buried there. He knew from past experience that Cholera could wipe out an entire wagon train. He also knew Cholera was not the only thing that killed many travelers as they crossed the open prairie. If he was to find out, he knew he had to read more. Joshua turned a couple of pages in the diary and started to read again.

*July 2nd 1856. Dear Diary, Another family on the wagon train became ill today. It is a shame they had to be moved away from the rest of us, but Mr. Moffett and some of the others say it is necessary to keep the sickness from spreading to everyone else. It was the second wagon to be driven off this week. I am sure Mr. Moffett will have us continue on in the morning without them. It breaks my heart to have to leave them behind. I wish there was something I could do to help them, but Mr. Moffett says I need to stay away from them so I do not get the sickness, too. Jenny.*

Joshua looked up from the diary and thought about what he had read. He was convinced the wagon train had had an outbreak of Cholera. If that was the case, there was a strong possibility the people who had been in the wagon he was sitting in had been driven away from the wagon train for that same reason.

Joshua couldn't help but think about Jenny. She had to be someone very special. She sounded like someone who would do anything to help others. He looked back at the diary and turned a couple of more pages.

*July 5th 1856. Dear Diary, My heart is full of sadness. Three more families have come down with the sickness. Mr. Moffett has ordered all the families to stay close to their wagons and not to mix with any other family. The people are scared, but I cannot blame them. I am scared, too. It does make it hard for some. Jobs that were once shared to make them easier for everyone now have to be done without the help of others. As I was sitting on the seat of the wagon, I could see the Sutter's wagon far behind us. They were the last to be driven away from the wagon train. Mr. Sutter was angry and told Mr. Moffett that he would follow him all the way to Oregon if he had to. He said he was not going to be left out on the prairie to die like some of the others. After dark I could see their fire next to the wagon. Mr. Sutter was the only one I saw by the fire. I do not know if the others were sick or if they had gone to bed. It is late and Mr. Moffett said we would be moving again at daybreak. Jenny.*

Joshua read the diary with growing interest. Not only did he notice what steps Mr. Moffett had taken in the hope of preventing or at least slowing down the spread of the disease, but he also noticed Jenny was now signing her diary without saying "Goodnight". He was sure what had been happening was taking its toll on everyone, including her. Joshua continued to read.

*July 6th 1856. Dear Diary, We did not get very far today. The weather was warm and sunny, but we had to cross a river that flowed down to the Platte. It took time for all of us to get across. The place where we crossed was muddy and steep. Two of the wagons got stuck and had to be pulled out with the help of several extra teams of oxen. One wagon got sideways on the steep bank and turned over. It took a lot of work and time to get it right again. Once we were across the river, Mr. Moffett told everyone they should make sure their animals got plenty to eat and plenty of rest. He said from here on it was going to get even harder. The Sutters are still following along behind the wagon train. They are still on the other side of the river. I hope they can get across by themselves as no one here will go back to help them. There was an argument between several of the men and Mr. Moffett about the way he was handling things. A few of the men did not like the fact that Mr. Sutter was still following along behind. They thought that he was too close and could still spread the disease to them, but Mr. Moffett said as long as Mr. Sutter kept his distance he would not do anything about it. I noticed several men are standing guard near the river to make sure Mr. Sutter does not try to cross the river until we have moved on. Jenny.*

Joshua knew what she was talking about. He had seen enough of such things in the years he had been a Wagon Master on the Oregon Trail. The trip was hard and many didn't make it to the Promised Land. Some were unable to maintain a positive attitude, and some didn't understand the hardships they would face on such a long and difficult journey. And, of course, some died along the way.

Joshua was getting a sense of what was happening on the wagon train, but he still didn't understand why the wagon was where it was, and what had happened to the people that had been in it. He began reading the diary again.

*July 7th 1856. Dear Diary, Today was a day that I will never forget for as long as I live. At first light, Mr. Moffett started the wagon train moving again. Since we were near the end and one of the last ones to start moving, I could look back down the long low hill toward the river we had crossed yesterday. I could see Mr. Sutter trying to get his wagon across the river so he could follow us. Even from a long way away, I could see he had gotten his wagon stuck in the mud. While trying to pull the wagon out of the mud, the oxen turned. Mr. Sutter's wagon turned and rolled over into the river. I could see Mrs. Sutter fall from the wagon into the water. I called for somebody to go back and help them, but no one would listen. They would not even turn around and look. I cannot believe that no one would go help them. I never felt so helpless, so upset and angry with the others, and so disappointed with myself.*

Joshua stopped reading, leaned back and closed his eyes. He could picture in his mind what was happening. All the people in the wagon train were looking forward and were not talking. They refused to look back for fear that if they did they would never be able to leave the Sutters in the river.

He felt Jenny had tried to get them to go back, but they were afraid. They were afraid if they went back they would get the sickness. Jenny found it difficult to understand why people do what they do and sometimes there is no reason. But one thing is for sure, and Joshua knew it well, fear is one of the strongest human emotions. It will do more to dictate what a person does more than almost anything else.

Joshua looked back at the diary and began reading from where he had left off.

*Almost no one talked for the rest of the day. I am sure they were all upset with themselves for leaving the Sutters to die. I found it hard to talk to father about it. I had always thought of him as a brave man, a kind man, but after this I do not know what to think. Jenny.*

Joshua could understand how she felt. It had to have been a shock to her to see the one man in her life she looked up to turning his back on someone in need of help. He knew it was survival that made him do what he did. Jenny may not have understood that, but Joshua was sure her father understood it. He turned the page and began reading again.

*July 8th 1856. Dear Diary, Today everyone seemed to be depressed. I talked with father this morning and he explained why no one would go help the Sutters. I had most of the day to think about what he told me. I think I am beginning to understand even if I do not entirely agree. During the day I noticed father looked a little pale. I asked him about it but he said he was just tired. He went to bed as early as he could. I sat by the fire and watched him. Billy was complaining of a headache and his stomach hurt, but mother said it was most likely too much sun and all the wild berries he had eaten. We found them in a ravine near our camp. It is late and time for me to turn in. Jenny.*

This was the part of the diary that told Joshua a lot of what he wanted to know. Jenny's father and brother were most likely coming down with the sickness. It would be only a matter of a day or two before they would be separated from the wagon train and forced to travel behind. He continued to read the diary. He noticed there was no entry for July 9th, 1856 and he wondered why. He would soon find out.

*July 10th, 1856. Dear Diary, Yesterday it was quiet in our wagon. Father was able to keep moving, but not without some difficulty. Today Father and Billy are very sick and Mr. Moffett saw them. Mr. Moffett told us that we would have to leave the wagon train for the sake of the others. At father's insistence, we took the wagon off the trail and down by the river. He said it would be cooler in among the cottonwood trees, and we would be closer to water. I have built a fire and keep a pot of hot water on the fire at all times. Mother has been at father's side all day. Billy has been sleeping most of the time. We tried to get them to eat something, a bit of broth, anything, but it is of little use. I have been tending to Billy, but all he does is sleep. At father's wish, I turned the oxen out to graze. I think he knows we are all going to spend our last days on earth right here. I took a few minutes to look around. It is not such a bad place to spend the last days of one's life. The leaves of the cottonwood trees flutter in the cool breeze. There are some big white clouds slowly moving across the blue sky. There are birds singing in the trees and the river flows by at a leisurely pace. It is very peaceful here. Jenny.*

Joshua found it interesting how Jenny described this place. He found he could not put the diary down even though he had a good idea what was going to happen from there.

*July 11th, 1856. Dear Diary, Billy has a fever and I cannot get it down. I carried him down to the river and laid him in the cool water, but it did not seem to help very much. Even the cool evening air did not help him. I fear we will lose him soon. Father is not* getting any better, either. He is still able to talk to mother, but he goes in and out of sleep. I can see the worry on mother's face. I am worried, too. Jenny.

July 12th 1856. Dear Diary, We lost Billy this morning. I had to dig his grave in the sand and bury him myself. Mother was in such a state that she could not handle it and father was too weak to help me. Mother sat with father and cried until no more tears would come. I made a little cross as a marker for Billy's grave and said a little prayer for him. I fear father is not going to recover from the sickness, either. He has a fever now and has not responded to mother since early morning. I fear we will be burying him in the morning if his fever does not break. Jenny.

July 13th 1856. Dear Diary, Father is still with us although he is not responding to anything. We have been trying to keep his fever down as much as we can, but nothing seems to work. Although mother has not said anything, I think she has the sickness, too. She has hardly eaten anything and she looks like *she might have a fever. Whenever I suggest she rest, she turns me away and says father needs her. Jenny.*

*July 14th, 1856. Dear Diary, Father has given up and has gone to a better place, but it seems mother has taken his place here. She is running a fever and feels sick to her stomach. She was so sick she could not help me bury father. I dug another grave next to Billy's and laid him to rest there. I made a cross out of a couple of cottonwood sticks and put it at the head of the grave. I read a prayer from the Good Book for him and hope he will rest in peace with Billy. I fear it will not be long before mother will join him. She is not strong and I doubt she will be able to fight off the sickness. I am tired, but I will do all I can to make mother as comfortable as possible for as long as I can. We are running low on food. I will not be able to leave to hunt, as mother will need me. I will try to get some rest now and worry about what there is to eat in the morning. Jenny.*

*July 15th, 1856. Dear Diary, Mother was weak and did not last the night. I buried her with father this morning, as I know it is where she would want to be. I read a prayer for her and made a cross for her grave as well. I do not know what I will do now. As I sit here, I looked around. I am very much alone. The oxen have wondered off and I do not know where they have gone. The horse we had has also wandered off and I have no idea which way he went. I am about out of food. I will rest tonight and think about what I will do in the morning. Jenny.*

Joshua just looked at the diary. All of them had died except for the girl. He looked outside the wagon and wondered where she might have gone. If he looked around, would he find her body somewhere nearby? It had been over two months since she had been left alone with no one to help her.

It was getting dark and there was nothing he could do now. He decided he would get a good night's rest and spend a couple of days looking for her. Joshua had little hope of finding her as she could have gone in any direction, and in over two months, she could have gone some distance.

Then it hit him. Maybe her diary would give him some idea which way she had gone. He sensed she was a strong willed and a very determined young woman, but she had left her diary behind. He wondered why she did that. Was it her hope that someone would find it and eventually find her? He would think on it as it was getting too dark to read any more tonight. For now he would rest and think about it later.

When morning came, Joshua got up and built himself a fire. Before he started to prepare himself a pot of coffee, a slab of bacon, and some biscuits for his breakfast, he hobbled his horses in a patch of thick green grass so they could graze.

He was squatted down to turn over the bacon in the pan when he heard something splashing in the river. He turned and looked over his shoulder to see five Indian braves coming across the river, but he was not afraid. He had become friends with the tribe these Indians came from and he recognized a couple of the braves. Joshua raised his hand in greeting and invited them to join him for some coffee. The warriors squatted down around the fire.

"Good to see you, Running Deer. What brings you so far from your village?" he asked one of the young braves in their native language.

"It is good to see you, Joshua. We have been hunting and saw your fire," the brave replied.

"Can you tell me anything about this wagon?" Joshua asked.

"The people that were in this wagon had the sickness. They died, all but one. A girl."

"Do you know where the girl is?"

"She is in our village."

"Is she well?"

"Yes."

"Where is your village?"

"About two days ride north. Do you wish to go there and see this girl?"

"Yes."

"Good. My father will be glad to see you. It has been many moons since you have been in our village."

Joshua and his friends finished eating and drinking the coffee. When they were through, they said their goodbyes and went on down the river. Joshua packed his gear and headed north.

Two days later, Joshua entered the village and was greeted as a friend. Lone Eagle invited him to stay as long as he wanted and provided him with a teepee to stay in.

Joshua sat down with his friend Lone Eagle and explained why he was there and that he wanted to see the white girl. Lone Eagle agreed and had the white girl brought to his tent.

When she stepped into Lone Eagle's teepee, Joshua's jaw dropped. Jenny was a tall slender young woman with long brown hair and dark brown eyes. As soon as she saw Joshua, she smiled at him.

"You're Jenny?" he asked.

"Yes," she replied. "How is it you know my name?"

"I have something that belongs to you," Joshua said. Joshua got up and went to the teepee. He retrieved Jenny's diary from his saddle bags and returned to her. He handed her the diary. She looked surprised that he had it.

"I missed it," she said sadly. "I missed having it to write in."

"Why did you leave it behind?"

"I felt there were more important things I needed to take with me. I had to travel light."

"Can you tell me, what is your last name?"

"McCutchum, Jenny McCutchum," she said with a smile.

Joshua and Jenny spent the next few hours talking about what had happened on the wagon train and how she had gotten to the village. Joshua found out that after she had buried her mother, she had packed up what she could carry and started walking. She was found hungry and afraid by one of Lone Eagle's hunting parties. They took her back to the village with them where she had been living ever since. She told Joshua that they had treated her well.

After several days in the village, Joshua decided it was time for him to be on his way if he was going to get to Fort Cheyenne before winter set in. Jenny asked if she could go with him. He agreed after talking it over with Lone Eagle.

They spent the next couple of days getting things together for the trip to Fort Cheyenne. When they were ready, they said goodbye to Lone Eagle and his tribe and started out.

During the long days and nights it took them to reach Fort Cheyenne, Jenny and Joshua grew close. Shortly after arriving at Fort Cheyenne, Joshua and Jenny were married by the Army Chaplain. Soon after the wedding, they opened a trading post where they lived for several years. When the fort was closed, they started ranching, raising cattle on the open prairie near the old fort. During their years together they raised a family.

# THE RIVERBOAT GAMBLER

The River Queen, a paddle wheel riverboat, was docked on the bank of the Missouri River outside of Omaha. It was loaded with supplies that were going to the trading posts along the Missouri River. The boilers had been stoked and the riverboat had built up enough steam to begin the journey. The only thing left was for the passengers to get on board.

As the whistle blew a long single note to let everyone know that the River Queen was about to leave, two rather large men with deputy badges on their shirts were escorting a tall man toward the riverboat. The man was wearing a tall hat, a gray frock coat, a black vest and a white shirt with ruffles down the front. He wore shoes with white spats. When they arrived at the gangplank, the two sheriff's deputies shoved the man onto the gangplank and watched him as he stumbled aboard the riverboat.

"If'n you know what's good for yah, you won't be comin' back this a way," one of the deputies said.

"This isn't fair. I didn't do anything that should have upset the sheriff so much that he needs to run me out of town like a common criminal," the man protested.

"Nothin' 'cept cheatin'," the deputy laughed.

"You can't do this," the gambler protested again.

"Maybe not, but we just did," the deputy said as he tossed the gamblers carpetbag onto the riverboat.

The gambler looked at the two deputies before he picked up his carpetbag. He didn't want to take the riverboat, but he had no choice.

As the gambler turned around, he found himself face to face with the riverboat's Captain. He looked into the big man's eyes and smiled.

"Excuse me, sir, but could you tell me where my cabin is?"

"Second deck, cabin number five," the Captain said flatly.

"Thank you."

"Mr. Wickham, I want to make it very clear right from the start. Gambling is permitted aboard my riverboat. However, cheating is not. If you are caught cheating, you WILL be tossed off my riverboat wherever we are. So there's no misunderstanding what I'm telling you, that includes in the middle of the river. Do I make myself clear?"

"Very clear, but I was not cheating at the Golden Eagle Saloon. I was framed," he said. "I do not have to cheat."

"Be that as it may, there will be no cheating on my riverboat."

"I understand," Oliver Wickham said, then walked past the Captain and started for the ladder to the second deck.

When Oliver reached the top of the ladder, he noticed a well dressed woman watching him. She was slim and nicely shaped. She was wearing a dress that was narrow at the waist with a full skirt that had to have a good number of petticoats under it. Her dark brown hair hung in ringlets to her shoulders and her brown eyes sparkled in the light of the nearby lamps. The smile on her face was as pleasant a smile as he had seen in a very long time.

"Good morning," Oliver said as he reached up, tipped his hat and bowed slightly.

"Good morning," she replied with a smile. "I noticed you had an escort."

"Ah, well, yes. It was most unfortunate that someone saw fit to accuse me of cheating during a card game last evening. I wasn't, but it didn't seem to matter to the sheriff."

"I see," the woman replied still with a smile on her face.

"It's true. It seems I made the mistake of playing cards with the mayor of this fair community. He wasn't much of a card player and I took him for a great deal of money. Not really wanting to admit that he had lost a lot of money and that he was a terrible poker player, he accused me of cheating and had the sheriff run me out of town," Oliver explained. "It seems this riverboat was the first and quickest way to get me out of town."

"I'm sure that's the reason," the young woman said.

"I'm really sorry you don't seem to believe me. I was hoping to get to know you. It's a long trip to Fort Pierre."

"I'm sure we will have a chance to talk again. Right now I would like to go to my cabin, if you don't mind?"

"Sorry," he replied as he stepped aside and let her pass by him.

Oliver watched the woman as she walked toward the front of the riverboat. He was going to get to know her before she got off the riverboat, he told himself.

He turned and walked down the deck to his cabin. The cabin was fairly small, but then the riverboat was not as big as some he had been aboard on the Mississippi River.

Oliver was tired as he had been up almost all night. He took off his coat and put it over the back of the chair, then set his hat on the small dresser. He laid down on the bed. He yawned and closed his eyes. Oliver needed some sleep and this was a good time to get it. It wasn't long before he was sound asleep.

It was late afternoon when Oliver woke up. He could hear the sound of the paddle wheels as they churned through the water. Oliver had no idea how far they had gone, but he doubted that it had been very far. He knew a person could move faster by horseback, but could not move as many supplies.

Oliver got up, washed his face, combed his hair and shaved. When he was done, he put on a clean shirt. As soon as he was ready, he left his cabin and went to the dining room where he had a good meal. When he was finished, he sat back and watched some men playing poker.

It appeared they were playing some serious poker with a good deal of money on the table. Oliver watched the players. He quickly became aware that each of them had signs they were giving, but the others were not picking up on them.

As soon as he felt he had studied the players long enough to know what to look for, Oliver stood up and went over to the table. He stood next to the table behind an empty chair and watched while the players finished the hand.

"You mind if I join you fellas?" he asked when they completed the hand.

Each of the players looked at one another. Then the one who was holding the cards looked up at Oliver.

"Not at all. I'm Marcus Billard, this here is Frank Sutton, and that big guy is Jess Kelman."

"I'm Oliver Wickham," he replied as he looked around the table.

Jess was a big man. He was probably in his late thirties or early forties. He had to be close to three hundred pounds and had big hard looking hands. His hair was dark and he wore a plaid shirt and denim pants. His nose had obviously been broken several times and his face showed the scars of many fights.

Frank appeared to be the youngest of the three. His dark hair was neatly trimmed and his clothes were clean and pressed. He was of medium build and had a ruddy complexion.

Marcus was the oldest of the three. He was in his late fifties. His hair was gray as was his mustache. He was neat and clean in appearance, and seemed to be alert to what was going on around him.

"We play straight poker, no fancy stuff," Jess said without any emotion in his voice.

"That's fine with me."

"We play five card draw, nothing wild. You get five cards and one chance to trade up to four new cards," Frank added.

"That sounds like the way I like to play," Oliver said as he pulled out the chair and sat down.

"By the way, we don't take to cheating around here. If you can't win fair and square, you might as well get up and leave now," Marcus said, the look on his face showing he was serious.

Oliver acknowledged with a slight nod of his head and reached inside his coat for a stack of bills. He counted out five hundred dollars and stacked the money on the table.

Oliver watched the dealer out of the corner of his eye as he tossed a five-dollar bill into the center of the table. It was a signal he was in for the next deal.

The first round of cards was dealt out by Jess. Oliver waited until all the cards had been dealt before picking his up. Oliver watched as each of the players picked up and sorted their cards. He watched them closer than he watched his own hand. After a number of bids and calls around the table, Oliver had managed to win the first hand. As the evening progressed, Oliver began to build his stack of cash.

While cards were being dealt, he noticed the woman he had met earlier had come into the room. He watched her as she sat down, but turned his attention back to the game.

Oliver lost a hand here and there, but most of the time he was winning. Occasionally, he would glance over at the woman and find her watching him.

It wasn't long and Oliver had a good deal of the players' money. The more he won, the angrier Jess seemed to get. The one who had lost the most money during the evening was Jess.

Suddenly, the big man slammed his cards down on the table and pushed his chair back as he stood up. He was a rather intimidating man when he was standing up. He looked down at Oliver with anger in his eyes.

"We told you we don't like cheaters," Jess said, as he stood there with his feet set and his hand ready to reach for his gun.

"I didn't cheat, and you know it," Oliver said calmly.

"Come on, Jess. He ain't been cheatin'. I've been watching him. He ain't done nothin' but take your money fair and square."

"You mind your own business, Frank," Jess retorted sharply.

"You don't want to do anything foolish, mister. I didn't cheat. You just shouldn't be playing cards for money," Oliver said quietly so as not to make the situation worse.

"What do you mean by that?" Jess asked, demanding an answer.

Oliver could see he better pick his words very carefully. To come out and tell him that he was giving away his hand every time he had good cards might prove to be the wrong thing to say. It wasn't that Oliver was afraid of him. It was he didn't want to have to shoot him over a card game.

"You're not the only one who has lost money. We've all lost money to this gambler fella," Marcus said.

"See, I told yah he was cheatin', Marcus," Jess said, feeling he now had someone to back him up.

"That ain't so. I was just about to pick up what money I had left cause I realized this fella could read us," Marcus said to clarify what he meant.

"You mean you know'd all along he was cheatin' us?" Jess asked Marcus.

"He weren't cheatin'. He was readin' us. He could tell if we had a good hand just by lookin' at us."

Jess seemed really confused by what Marcus had said. He didn't understand what was going on, but he felt like he had been cheated out of his money and that was good enough for him.

"That's still cheatin', ain't it Frank?" Jess asked as he turned to his other friend for support.

"No, it ain't," Frank answered. "He's just a lot smarter than us. He knows what to look for."

"Well, I want my money back and I intend to get it back."

"Jess, let it go. He done beat us fair and square," Marcus insisted.

"I still say it's cheatin'," Jess persisted.

Oliver was ready for whatever Jess was going to do. He hoped Jess would give it up, but he had seen men like him before. They set their mind to something and couldn't give it up.

"Mister, you took us fair and square," Frank said. "I'll remember you and won't sit down at a table to play cards with you again."

Marcus stood up and took his remaining money off the table. As he turned to leave, he stopped and looked back at Oliver.

"You're one smart gambler, young fella. You done taught me a lesson I won't soon forget. It was a costly lesson, and I'll not forget it."

Oliver nodded he understood, but didn't take his eyes off Jess. As far as he was concerned, Jess was still a threat. To ignore him was to end up dead.

At that moment, the Captain came into the room with two other men. He walked over to the table and looked down at Oliver.

"We told you that we were not going to have any cheating on my riverboat. Stand up," he ordered.

"Wait a minute," the young woman said as she stood up and started across the room.

"Ma'am, this is none of your concern. Please go back to your table," the Captain said politely.

"But it is my business. He was not cheating. Even this man's friends will admit he was not cheating. He is very good at cards and these gentlemen, well, are not. This gentleman is – ah – well, he's a poor loser."

"Ma'am, . . . ," he started to say but was interrupted.

"The lady's right, sir."

The Captain turned and saw Marcus standing behind him.

"What do you know about this?"

"I was playin' at the table with this gambler fella. He took me for a lot of money, but he didn't cheat none. He's just a damn sight better player than the rest of us. What he took from us, he done fair and square."

Jess looked at Marcus and the lady, then turned and looked at Oliver. He then looked up at the Captain.

"I guess I have to let you go," the Captain said to Oliver then turned toward Jess.

"As for you, I suggest you don't play cards with this man any more. And if you cause me any more trouble, I'll see to it you're dealt with accordingly. Do you understand that?"

"Yes," Jess replied reluctantly.

"Now, go about your business," the Captain said to Jess.

Jess took one last look at Oliver. He was not happy with how things had turned out, not one bit happy about it. He picked up what money he had left and stormed out of the room.

Oliver watched as Jess left. It was over, but Oliver wondered for how long. If he knew anything about human nature, he knew Jess was not the kind of a man to let it go. Oliver was sure he would have a confrontation with Jess again.

"I'll be keeping an eye on you," the Captain said to Oliver, then turned and left.

Oliver turned and looked at the young woman. He reached up and tipped his hat to her. She nodded slightly and returned to her table.

After collecting his money, Oliver walked across the room to where the woman was sitting.

"Thank you for standing up for me," he said as he took his hat off.

"You're quite welcome. I was watching you play. You didn't cheat. From the looks of it, you didn't have to," she said with a smile.

"No, Ma'am', I didn't," he said. "My name is Oliver Wickham."

"Mary Sutherland," she replied. "Would you like to sit down?"

"Thank you," he replied as he pulled out a chair and sat down across the table from her.

"Is it Miss or Mrs.?"

"It's Mrs."

"And where might Mr. Sutherland be?"

"Actually, it's Captain Sutherland. He is an officer in the U.S. Army and stationed at Fort Randall. I'm going to join him there."

"I see," Oliver said, disappointed that she was married.

"That was rather close. I thought that man was going to shoot you."

"He might have tried," Oliver said calmly.

"Doesn't it bother you that he might have killed you?" she asked, the look on her face showing how confused she was by his lack of concern.

"I doubt he would have been able to kill me. You see, I had a gun under the table. It was pointed right at him," he said, in an effort to show her that he had been prepared for the worst.

"I see," she said not sure she believed him. "I think it's time to call it a night."

"You're probably right. Would you like me to walk you to your cabin?" Oliver asked.

"No, thank you. I can find my way," she replied politely, but with a tone of firmness he had not expected.

"Very well. In that case, I'll say goodnight."

Oliver stood up, picked up his hat and left the room. As he stepped out the door onto the deck, he glanced back over his shoulder to take one last look at Mrs. Sutherland. It crossed his mind that he would have liked to get to know her better if it wasn't for the fact she was married.

Oliver walked down the deck toward the ladder that would take him up to the second deck of the riverboat. As he put his hand on the rail and raised his foot to take the first step up the ladder, he heard the faint sound of a gun hammer cocking behind him. He quickly pulled himself off to the side and dove for cover behind a large wooden crate.

He had no more then hit the deck when a shot rang out. The bullet hit the edge of the crate and caused splinters to fly all over the place.

Oliver returned fire with one shot from the small pistol he carried under his arm inside his coat. The bullet did not hit anyone, but it came close. The next thing he heard was the sound of someone running toward the rear of the riverboat.

It had been dark so Oliver had not gotten a chance to see who had tried to bushwhack him. He didn't think he really needed to see who it was. There was only one person aboard the riverboat that was out to get him.

As Oliver stood up, the Captain and a couple of the crew came running down the deck toward him. They had guns in their hands and were ready for a fight.

"What happened here? It's you again," the Captain said in disgust.

"Someone took a shot at me. If I hadn't heard him cock his gun, he would have gotten me."

"Well, I'm not surprised. You took those men for a good deal of money."

"Maybe I did, but I did it legally and without cheating," Oliver said with a tone of anger in his voice. "What are you going to do about it?"

"I think the best thing to do is to toss you off my riverboat," the Captain said calmly.

"You can't do that. I haven't done anything," Oliver protested.

"I don't want any trouble on my riverboat. You seem to be the cause of the trouble. That's enough for me to toss you off."

"We're in the middle of nowhere. How am I supposed to get to some place where I can get a horse or other transportation?"

"That, sir, is your problem."

The Captain turned around and told one of the crew to get Oliver's belongings. The Captain then gave orders for the pilot to move the riverboat over close to the shore.

Oliver didn't say anything more. The Captain was not interested in justice. He was only interested in having peace on his riverboat.

When the crewmember returned with Oliver's carpet-bag, the Captain took it and handed it to him. Oliver took it and walked over to the gangplank that had been lowered. As the riverboat came close to the shore, Oliver stood on the gangplank.

"If you go down the road, you'll find a farm house. The man that owns the farm may be willing to sell you a horse," the Captain said. "But I wouldn't be disturbing the farmer until after daybreak, if I was you."

Oliver did not say anything. He simply walked to the end of the gangplank and jumped off onto the riverbank. He turned and watched as the riverboat slowly moved back out toward the middle of the river.

Oliver started walking down the narrow road. When he came to a large old tree next to the road, he leaned his carpetbag against the tree and laid down. He rested his head on the carpetbag to get some sleep.

When morning came, Oliver went to the farmhouse the Captain had told him about. It took him only a few minutes to get the farmer to sell him a horse and saddle. It wasn't long before Oliver was on his way to the next place where the riverboat was to dock. In fact, he was waiting for the riverboat when it arrived.

The riverboat's whistle blew to let everyone know it was coming in to tie up. Oliver was sitting behind a stack of crates where he could not be seen by anyone on the riverboat. By the time anyone would see him, they would have walked past him.

He could hear the Captain giving orders to his crew. He heard the Captain announce that they would be tied up for two hours while they took on fuel. During that time, anyone could go ashore, if they wanted.

Oliver was watching to see if Jess would get off the riverboat. If Jess didn't get off here, Oliver would follow him to the next place the riverboat was scheduled to put in. He saw Jess step up on the gangplank.

Oliver was an easygoing man, but even easygoing men have their limits. His limits were having someone shoot at him from ambush. The fact that he had to walk several miles, sleep on the cold, damp ground and pay for a horse and saddle he didn't want was part of it, too. Jess was not going to get away with it.

Jess was walking with Frank and Marcus toward a saloon a short distance from the river. As they walked by Oliver, he stood up and readied himself for a confrontation.

"Hello, Jess," he said in a tone that wasn't threatening.

Jess stopped in his tracks, but didn't turn around. Jess had immediately recognized Oliver's voice.

Frank and Marcus turned around first and saw Oliver standing there. They slowly moved away from Jess. They wanted no part of this fight.

Slowly, Jess started to turn around. The look on his face showed he was afraid Oliver had the drop on him. But when he didn't see a gun in Oliver's hand, he relaxed a little.

"I don't take kindly to being shot at by some coward who hasn't guts to face me," Oliver said watching Jess's eyes.

It angered Jess to be called a coward. His jaw tightened and his breathing became more rapid.

"You want to try again now that I can look you in the eye?" Oliver asked.

"Mister, I don't want no trouble," Jess said as he took a step back.

"I didn't want any trouble either, but you got me tossed off the riverboat. I ended up having to buy a horse and saddle that I didn't want. And I also lost a nice comfortable cabin to sleep in and had to sleep under a tree on the ground. Now what do you think we should do about that?"

"Jess, I think you ought to pay him for the horse and saddle and a little extra for the cabin," Frank suggested.

"Yeah. I think that's a good idea," Marcus agreed.

By now, Jess had had a chance to look Oliver over. He couldn't see that he even had a gun. He had not seen one on the riverboat, and he didn't see one now.

"I ain't paying him nothin'," Jess said defiantly.

"You ain't?" Oliver asked, mocking him.

"No, I ain't. And I don't see how you're big enough to make me," Jess said.

Jess was not very bright. He hadn't figured out that Oliver had to have had a gun somewhere under his coat. How else would he have been able to fire back at him on the boat?

"Listen little man, I ain't payin' you nothin'. Now if you think you're man enough to take me, you're welcome to try."

"I'm not one to fight another man over a few dollars, but since you shot at me I'll gladly make an exception," Oliver said.

Jess began to grin from ear to ear. He was a lot bigger than Oliver and appeared to be much stronger.

"Take off the gun," Oliver said.

"I don't need a gun to kill you. I can do it with my bare hands," he said as he reached for the buckle on his gun belt.

Oliver watched him as he took off his gun belt. Jess handed it to Frank and then turned to face Oliver. He quickly noticed Oliver had not taken off his fancy coat.

"Ain't you goin' to take off that fancy coat of your'n? You might get it dirty."

Oliver didn't say a word. He simply reached inside his coat, pulled out his gun and pointed it at Jess' face. The look on Jess' face was priceless.

"I have no doubt you could probably beat me within an inch of my life, but I'm not going to give you the chance. You are going to pay me four hundred dollars for the horse, the saddle, the cabin I didn't get to use and for the uncomfortable night I spent on the ground. Do I make myself clear?"

Jess stood there with his mouth hanging open. It took a minute or two for him to realize that Oliver had beaten him again.

Reluctantly, Jess reached into his pocket and pulled out what was left of his bankroll. He had already lost most of it last night, now he was about to lose some more. The idea didn't set well with him, but he didn't see that he had much choice in the matter.

Jess counted out four hundred dollars and held it out to Oliver. Knowing it was not safe to reach out and take it, Oliver had him set the money on a barrel nearby, then back away.

Oliver did not take his eyes off Jess as he backed up close to his friends. Oliver moved over to the barrel and picked up the money. In the split second Oliver had taken to glance over and pick up the money, Jess grabbed for the gun in Frank's holster.

Someone yelled, "Look out!" and Oliver quickly jumped to one side as he turned in time to see Jess pulling Frank's gun out of his holster. Oliver fired one quick shot at Jess. His bullet hit the big man in the chest.

Jess had a surprised look in his eyes. He looked down at the front of his shirt and saw the blood stain as it grew larger. Jess looked back at Oliver, stumbled a little and then fell on his face in the dirt.

It was over in less than a minute. Jess was dead on the ground.

Oliver looked at the big man for a minute or so, then turned and walked toward his horse. As he walked away, he saw the young woman he had talked to on the riverboat. The look on her face told him all he needed to know. She had been the one that yelled out the warning.

"Thank you," he said as he walked by.

Oliver got on his horse, took a quick look over his shoulder at the young woman, then turned around and rode on down the road.

# THE MOUNTAIN MAN

A lone man with a pack on his back was walking along a narrow trail. He had a flintlock musket in his hand and was wearing buckskin clothing and a coonskin cap. His high-top moccasins had fringe around the top and a long thin dagger was neatly tucked in the top of the right one. In his belt he carried a flintlock pistol and a sharp hunting knife. Swung across his shoulder were his powder horn and a pouch that held his shot, patches and flints.

The man's hair was long and dark with hints of gray on the sides. He had a full beard that concealed the scars from the many fights he had had with Indians. His eyes were green and sparkled with life in the morning sun.

Zebadiha Jones was a mountain man. He lived off the land while he trapped and hunted for furs and hides. He had lived off the land for many years.

The trail he had been following ran along a creek that wound from the plains up into the Southern Black Hills and on into a valley.

The meadow had two beaver dams that formed two large ponds.

Zebadiha was a cautious man, his life depended on it. As he entered the valley, he stayed back in the trees as he scouted the valley and looked over the meadow.

The meadow was thick with long grass and wild flowers. Thick woods surrounded the meadow that was almost two miles long and about a half mile wide.

He looked up at the sky. If he was lucky and got to work right away, and the snows of winter held off for a while, he might have a chance to set up a permanent camp. He would be able to find plenty of food, and he would be able to trap for furs. There was good timber for a cabin.

By the time Zebadiha had made a complete circle of the meadow, he knew the valley would provide him with everything he would need to live there. There was no doubt in his mind that the valley would be a good place to spend the winter.

Zebadiha needed to build a shelter that would provide him with protection from the weather while he settled into the valley. He began by building a shelter for the night in among the trees. When he was done, he built a small fire and made himself a pot of coffee. He sat down next to the fire and ate hard tack and jerky. Tomorrow he would go hunting so that he would have some fresh meat.

\* \* \* \*

Days passed into weeks, and weeks into months. Zebadiha split his time between building himself a small cabin with a sod roof, hunting for food and skins, and trapping a few beaver. He hauled rocks to his cabin site from the nearby stream and used mud from the creek mixed with dried grass to make mortar for a fireplace and chimney. He sealed the spaces between the logs of his cabin with mortar so there would be no drafts. The ceiling beams were only five and a half feet above the floor, but that was enough since Zebadiha was only five foot five inches tall. He removed the sod from inside the cabin to get down to solid dirt for his floor and used the sod on the roof.

After Zebadiha finished his cabin, he painstakingly cut the wood to make a door strong enough to keep large animals out.

After hanging the door, he stood back and looked at his handiwork. The cabin was solid, cozy, and would provide him with protection from his enemies as well as shelter from the cold of winter that would soon be upon him.

Zebadiha then set to making a bench and a table where he could eat his meals and do many of the hundreds of other little tasks he would have to do just to live from day to day. He laid out logs on the floor to form a bed and filled the space with dry leaves and grass. He covered it with oilcloth and a buffalo hide to make his bed.

He worked from sunup to sundown every day, seven days a week without fail. He had to in order to get everything done so he could survive the harsh Dakota Territory winter. He had put up a supply of firewood and dried meat. He also gathered nuts and other edibles from the forest when he could. He cleaned the fur from the beavers he trapped, and tanned the hides of the deer, elk and buffalo. He dried some of the meat to help get through the winter if the snow was too deep for him to go out and hunt.

He wasted nothing, not even the bones of the larger animals, which he turned into spoons, forks, and other tools for daily living. There was no time for anything but work. It was a hard life being a mountain man, but it was his life.

* * * *

Early one morning in late October, Zebadiha woke from his sleep. It was colder than usual. He got up and wrapped his buffalo robe around his shoulders as he walked over to the fireplace. He added wood to the fire and brought the fire back to life. The fire began to warm the small cabin.

He dressed and fixed himself some breakfast. When he was done eating, he put on the buffalo coat he had made and opened the door to his cabin. He was surprised to see it had snowed during the night. In fact, it was still snowing lightly.

He stood in the doorway and looked out over the meadow. The ground was completely covered with an inch or more of snow. It had turned cold rather quickly, but Zebadiha had been expecting it. He was ready for winter.

The ponds were not frozen over, although they did have some ice around the edges. He would still be able to get to his traps without having to cut through ice.

The one thing Zebadiha didn't like about the snow was the fact that he would leave a trail wherever he went. That meant he would have to be very careful. Every place he went would be recorded in the snow until it either melted or it snowed again and covered his tracks.

The snow also had a good side. It would tell him what kinds of animals were moving around in the valley. It would also tell him if anyone had come into the valley.

Zebadiha decided he would not go directly to the ponds to check on his beaver traps. Instead, he would circle around and see what kinds of critters were moving around in the early morning hours.

He reached over next to the door and picked up his powder horn and shot pouch. He slipped them over his shoulder, picked up his rifle and left the cabin.

He kept his eyes moving, continually checking the meadow from the edge of the forest. He watched for any kind of movement in the forest. He would stop every once in awhile to look and listen. The forest had sounds of its own. Zebadiha would listen for sounds that did not belong in the forest and for sounds he could not identify. All he could hear was the tapping sound of a woodpecker on a tree and the occasional songs of other birds.

When he came to the end of the meadow, he looked into the narrow opening where the creek wound its way out of the valley. Zebadiha stood hidden by a large Ponderosa Pine as he carefully scanned both sides of the creek. He was looking for tracks that would let him know if anyone had come into the valley.

Once he was satisfied no one had come into the meadow from the eastern end, he began walking toward the creek. He crossed over the narrow creek and slipped back into the forest.

As he began to move west through the woods, he noticed there were indents in the snow that were evenly spaced. The indents were too far apart to have been made by a man walking. They indicated to him some kind of animal had walked through the snow before it had stopped snowing.

He stopped, knelt down for a closer look. Zebadiha was not sure what kind of an animal had made them. The tracks were too big to have been made by a deer, and the distance between the tracks ruled out a mountain lion.

Based on what he could make out, he believed that either a horse or a buffalo had made the tracks. The thought it might be a horse worried him. Although he was unable to determine what kind of an animal it was, he was able to tell which way the animal had gone.

If it was a buffalo, it was a rather large one. If he could find it, it would provide him with lots of meat and another hide he could use during the cold winter. He decided he would follow the tracks.

Zebadiha looked off in the direction the tracks seemed to be going. Since the tracks were going in the same direction he had planned to go, following them for awhile would do no harm.

He stood up and started walking along side the tracks. The thought that there might be someone else in the valley made Zebadiha stay alert.

He followed the tracks for almost a mile when he saw something move in among the trees. Zebadiha took cover behind a tree to watch. When the animal moved again, he was able to get a good look at it. He was surprised to see a brown and white Indian pony with a red blanket on its back. But what concerned him the most was the fact that there was no Indian on the horse and no Indian in sight. He wondered where the horse had come from, but more importantly where was the rider.

Zebadiha's mind was working hard to figure out what he should do. All he knew was if there was an Indian pony, there had to be an Indian somewhere.

He again looked at the horse. The horse didn't seem to be going anywhere. Yet, its tracks had showed it had been moving along as if it had some destination in mind. To a man like Zebadiha, that didn't make any sense.

The horse didn't seem to be concerned about its surroundings. He appeared to be calm and relaxed. It was as if he had been there before.

Zebadiha started slowly working his way toward the horse. He moved from one tree to the next, stopping often to look around to make sure he was not walking into a trap.

Just as he was about to catch the horse, he caught a glimpse of something out of the corner of his eye. He froze in his tracks then slowly turned his head in an effort to see what had caught his attention.

Zebadiha stared at a red and black Indian blanket partially hidden by a large tree. The blanket appeared to match the one on the horse. Staring at the blanket, he thought it looked as if there might be someone wrapped up in it and leaning against the tree.

He began moving toward it so he could get a better look. He soon discovered there was someone wrapped in the blanket. He could not see a face, but he could see a single feather sticking out from under the blanket.

It had turned cold last night and Zebadiha wondered if the Indian got caught unprepared. There was always the possibility he had gotten lost and settled in to wait out the snow.

Zebadiha moved a little closer to see if the Indian was alive. He moved closer and closer to the blanket making sure he kept his gun ready at all times.

When he got close, the horse let out a whinny. Zebadiha froze in his tracks and waited to see if the Indian was going to move. He did not move.

Zebadiha leaned his rifle against a tree and drew his pistol from his belt. With his pistol in one hand, he reached out and carefully pulled the blanket open. He found a young Indian brave hunched over under the blanket. The Indian did not move and his eyes were closed. At first, Zebadiha thought he was dead. Then he noticed the thin gray vapor coming from the brave's nose. He was still breathing. The young brave was alive, but just barely.

He knelt down beside the Indian and looked him over. He saw blood on the side of the young brave's head. It was clear that the Indian needed help, and needed it now. If the young brave were to survive, Zebadiha would have to take him to his cabin to warm him and treat his injuries.

Zebadiha looked around as he questioned the wisdom of taking an Indian into his cabin, but there was no one else to help him. It was up to him to either let the young brave die, or help him as best he could. Either way was a risk.

The brave's horse was standing off only a few feet away watching him. Zebidiha stood up slowly and tucked his pistol back in his belt. He moved very carefully toward the horse. At first the horse backed away. It was unsure about the white man. Zebadiha talked to the horse softly in an effort to reassure it that all was okay. The horse finally let Zebadiha reach out and take hold of the leather rope around its neck.

After tying the horse to a nearby tree, Zebadiha lifted the brave up, wrapped him in the blanket and laid him over the horse. He led the horse across the meadow to his cabin. There was no time to worry about tracks. If this brave was to survive, he needed to get him some place warm, and quickly.

When Zebadiha arrived at the cabin, he tied the horse to a tree next to the cabin then carried the brave inside. He laid him on his bed, covered him with a buffalo robe and built up the fire. It didn't take long for the fire to warm the cabin.

Zebadiha heated water and gathered some small pieces of cloth to dress the brave's wounds. While he was cleaning and dressing the brave's wounds, he discovered that he had a nasty wound on his leg as well as the one on his head.

When Zebadiha finished caring for the brave and there was nothing else he could do for him, he covered him again with the buffalo robe to keep him warm. Zebadiha made the brave as comfortable as he could. He had done all he could. Now it was time to wait to see if the young brave survived.

He sat and watched the brave for several minutes before going outside. Zebadiha cleared away a bit of snow so the horse could get at the grass underneath.

When he returned to the cabin, the brave was still not awake. However, he did seem to be breathing easier. For the first time, Zebadiha had hoped that the brave might survive. He only hoped that taking the brave into his cabin would not prove to have been a bad decision.

It was still morning and Zebadiha had work to do. He decided he would go check his traps. The Indian was not going anywhere. Zebadiha was sure his injuries would keep him down for sometime.

Zebadiha gathered his rifle and shot pouch and started off toward the ponds. He spent the next few hours gathering the beavers he had caught and resetting his traps.

On his way back to his cabin, he stopped at the edge of the woods to look around. He scanned the meadow looking for anyone who might have come into the valley, but saw no one.

He took a look at the sky and was glad to see the sky had cleared and it was warming. He hoped the warmer weather would melt away his tracks in the snow before anyone found them. He could see most of his tracks had already disappeared.

As he turned around to go into his cabin, he could see the Indian's horse eating the wet grass. The horse didn't seem to mind being there.

Zebadiha hung the beavers on a peg outside his cabin before going inside. The young brave was still not awake, although he did seem to be resting comfortably. He added a little wood to the fire to keep the cabin warm then went back outside to clean and prepare the beaver pelts.

While he was working, he kept one eye out for anyone who might be looking for the brave. When he was done with the pelts, he went back inside. The brave had still not moved. Zebadiha began fixing a pot of buffalo stew. As it cooked over the fire, he sat down at the table to work on a pair of pants he was making out of an elk hide. He was sewing the hide together using thin strips of elk hide and a piece of buffalo bone he had fashioned into a sharp needle. The pants were to help keep his legs dry when he knelt down in the snow or on the wet ground to check his traps.

The young brave opened his eyes and watched the man work on the pieces of leather. He tried to remember if he knew the white man, but could not remember. His head hurt and there was pain in his side and his leg.

He tried to think of what had happened to him, but it was all sort of a blur. He wasn't sure, but he felt the white man had saved his life. He again closed his eyes and rested.

Zebadiha continued his work. It was getting on toward time to eat when he again looked at the brave. He found him looking back at him.

"I see you are awake," Zebadiha said in Lakota, the language of the Sioux.

The brave looked at him, but didn't say anything. He wondered who the white man was who spoke his language.

"What is your name?" Zebadiha asked when he didn't get a response to his first comment.

The young brave was reluctant to answer. He was not sure about him, but it didn't seem that the white man was intending to do him any harm. He certainly would not have brought him here and cared for him if he was.

"Little Eagle," he finally answered.

"Are you hungry?"

"Yes," Little Eagle replied as he sat up in the bed.

The act of sitting up was painful, but he couldn't let it show. It would be a sign of weakness.

"Good. I have some buffalo stew," Zebadiha said with a smile as he stood up.

He went over to the fireplace and scooped up a bowl of stew. He took it to Little Eagle and handed him a spoon. The brave looked at the stew, then at Zebadiha.

Little Eagle began eating the stew. Zebadiha was pleased to see Little Eagle eat. To him it was a sign that Little Eagle would recover.

After they finished eating, they sat and talked. Actually, Zebadiha did most of the talking. It was hard for Little Eagle to except the kindness of a white man. Although he had never met a white man before, he had heard stories about them and what they did to Indians.

As the days passed, Little Eagle began to recover from his injuries. Remembering what had happened, he explained to Zebadiha that he had been attacked by a band of Indians from another tribe while hunting. Although he had been injured, he had escaped into the valley. His enemies had not followed him.

The weather had turned warm again and all the snow had melted away. Zebadiha continued to keep an eye out for anyone in the valley. He only hoped Little Eagle's enemies did not become his enemies.

Late one evening while Zebadiha was out in front of the cabin cleaning some fish, Little Eagle ventured out of the cabin. He still had a rather severe limp from the injury to his leg, but he was able to get around. He stood in the door and watched Zebadiha. Zebadiha looked up and smiled.

"I see you are getting around. How does your leg feel?"

"It is getting better. I should be able to leave soon."

Zebadiha looked at him. The smile on his face faded. He had grown to like Little Eagle and knew he would miss him. The thought crossed his mind that Little Eagle would tell his people about him. It would not take long, even out here in the wilderness, for the word to spread about a white man living in the Black Hills.

"When you leave, will you tell others I am here?"

"I will tell my father," Little Eagle said. "He will want to thank you for helping me."

"I would like it if no one knows I am here."

Little Eagle looked at him. It took a few minutes for him to understand what was really in Zebadiha's heart.

"If I do not tell my father, he will still know someone had helped me. My wounds are too bad for me to have survived without help. I will not lie to my father," Little Eagle insisted.

"I would not want you to lie to your father," Zebadiha said.

Nothing more was said about it. They ate their meal, then went to bed.

After a few more days, Little Eagle was ready to leave. Zebadiha helped Little Eagle up on the back of his horse. They said their goodbyes, then Little Eagle rode off toward the narrow draw where he had entered the valley.

As soon as he was gone, Zebadiha let out a sigh. He hoped no one would come to the valley, but he knew he would have to keep a close watch. If he had to leave, it would be in a hurry. Zebadiha returned to the work at hand.

The days passed without any sign of anyone coming into the valley. He continued to trap and hunt, but kept a watchful eye.

Little Eagle had been gone for more than a week. Zebadiha continued checking his traps on the northern most pond. He also continued to keep his eyes open.

* * * *

One day while Zebadiha was kneeling down to reset a beaver trap, an arrow came flying out of the trees and sliced him across the top of his hip. The glancing blow of the arrow broke the skin and struck bone causing him a great deal of pain.

Zebadiha grabbed for his pistol from his belt as he fell to the ground. He was able to get his pistol free and roll over in time to see an Indian rushing toward him with a knife in his hand. Zebadiha pointed the gun at the Indian and pulled the trigger. The gun went off with a loud bang and a cloud of smoke. The Indian grabbed his stomach and doubled over as he fell to the ground only a few feet from Zebadiha.

Zebadiha quickly stuffed his pistol back in his belt and grabbed up his rifle in time to see another Indian start to draw his bow back. He quickly leveled his rifle and fired. The lead ball hit the Indian in the chest, dropping him right were he stood.

Being caught out in the open was not good. Zebadiha ran as best he could toward the trees. It was not easy to run with the injury to his hip. If he didn't get to cover and find a place to hide quickly, he would be killed. He had to find a place that would at least give him time to reload his guns.

Zebadiha scrambled toward a log and dove over it. He took a quick look around as he reached for his pouch. He knew it was not a good place to stay. Zebadiha didn't see any more Indians, but he knew they were out there. He had killed two so quickly that it caused the others to be more cautious. He could hear coyote calls from time to time, but knew they were signals from one Indian to another. Probably signals for them to move in for the kill.

Zebadiha loaded both his pistol and his rifle as quickly as he could. It would be only a matter of time before the Indians would get him surrounded. If that happened, there was little hope for him to survive the day.

He thought about making a break for the cabin, but if he got inside they would try to burn it down. His cabin was good protection from wild animals, but not Indians. He also knew if he did survive his fight with the Indians, he would need his cabin to survive the winter.

Zebadiha kept his eyes moving. He was not only watching for signs of what the Indians were doing, but for a better place to defend himself.

Suddenly, there seemed to be Indians everywhere. They had decided to attack him from all sides at once. He managed to get two more good shots off before they overran him. Although he had been successful at killing one and wounding another during the second attack, he didn't have time to reload again.

In the melee that followed, Zebadiha managed to use his knife to get one of them before he was struck on the head. The blow to the head dazed him and he was no longer able to fight back.

The Indians swarmed over him, beating and kicking him. When they were satisfied that he could not fight back, they picked him up, relieved him of all his weapons and dragged him to a couple of trees. They stripped him to the waist and tied him spread eagle between the trees.

They poured cold water over him. The air was cold and the water was intended to make him suffer from the cold even more, but it revived him at first.

Zebadiha had heard about the kind of torture done to white men by some bands of Indians, but he was too dazed and hurting to understand what they had in mind for him. He had blood in one eye and the other was swollen almost closed from being hit and kicked in the face. His nose was broken and his ribs hurt. The water they had poured over him was starting to cause him to shiver.

One of the Indians came up close to him. He was glaring at Zebadiha with hate in his eyes. He was wondering how much torture the mountain man could stand before he would beg them to kill him.

Zebadiha watched him as he slowly reached down and drew a knife from his belt. It was a big knife, and looked like it was very sharp. With a slight smirk on his face, he stepped up closer to Zebadiha holding the knife so Zebadiha could see it clearly.

He was raising his knife toward Zebadiha's face when suddenly a surprised look came over the Indian's face. His eyes were big and his mouth fell open as he gasped for air. The Indian stepped back a little, dropped the knife and reached for his back. He staggered a few steps before he turned and fell to the ground. Zebadiha could see an arrow sticking out of the Indian's back.

Suddenly there were several loud bloodcurdling yells and a large number of Indians came rushing out of the trees. They were led by Little Eagle. He had come just in time to save the white man who had saved him.

The Indians who had attacked Zebadiha were outnumbered and ran for their lives. As the rest of Little Eagle's band chased the other Indians down and killed them, Little Eagle came over to Zebadiha and cut him loose. He helped Zebadiha to his cabin where he took care of his wounds.

"I want to thank you," Zebadiha said, his voice shaky and not real clear. "If you had not come when you did, they would have killed me. Why did you come back?"

"I came back with some things to help you get through the winter," he said with a smile.

At that moment a young Indian woman came into the cabin. She didn't say a word, but went straight to the fireplace and began fixing soup.

"Who is she?" Zebadiha asked.

"She is Speaks Softly. She will stay with you until you are well. She is my sister," Little Eagle said.

Zebadiha laid back and watched the young woman. He was tired and sore, his body aching all over from the beating he had received. He was too sore to do anything but rest. Speaks Softly help him to eat the soup she had made.

As he laid there recovering from his wounds, the band of Indians that had come to his rescue set up camp out in front of his cabin. They stayed for several days doing the chores that needed to be done. When they left, Speaks Softly stayed behind to continue to care for Zebadiha and to do some of his chores.

Over the next few weeks, Zebadiha grew to like having the woman around. They became friends. As soon as Zebadiha was able to work again, they worked side-by-side trapping beaver and hunting. They never talked about Speaks Softly leaving and returning to her village, but they talked about a future together.

Eventually, Speaks Softly agreed to take Zebadiha to her father. Zebadiha gave her father two of the horses that had belonged to the Indians who had attacked him, a buffalo hide, and two deerskins so he could marry Speaks Softly. They stayed in the village of Speaks Softly's tribe for three days before they were married.

Afterwards, Zebadiha and Speaks Softly returned to Zebadiha's cabin where they lived as man and wife for many years. They added to the cabin over the years as their family grew. When it was no longer profitable to live off beaver and other hides, they turned to raising cattle, vegetables and other crops in the valley in the Black Hills.

# GOTS TA PLAY FAIR

I was sittin' in the corner of the saloon mindin' my own business. My business bein' that of the town Sheriff. I had me a beer I'd been sippin' on for the better part of an hour. There was little else ta do on such a dreary day. It had rained for the past few days and it looked like more taday.

I was watchin' four fellas playin' poker. There wasn't much money on the table so I got ta thinkin' it was just a friendly game ta pass the time.

I took a few minutes ta study them fellas. One looked like he might be a cowboy. He was young and fair-haired. His clothes was a might dusty, and his boots was wore some. He was tall and a little too cocky for his own good. I also noticed he seemed ta be drinkin' pretty steady and had been for sometime.

The fella sittin' across the table from the cowboy was dressed like a businessman. Like one of them drummer fellas that works his way 'round the country sellin' thin's ta folks that can't get ta town much. From the looks of the wooden box sittin' next ta his chair, he was sellin' barbed wire. If I had ta guess, he was probably waitin' for the afternoon stage ta take him on ta the next town.

The third man was a little fella. He was watchin' the others kinda close, like he might be 'fraid they might see him do somethin' he shouldn't be doin'. He tended ta watch the fourth fella sittin' across the table from him some closer than the others.

The fourth fella was all duded up in fancy clothes and sweet smellin' stuff. He was a might handsome fella, I guess. At least 'ccordin' ta what some of the women folks was sayin'. He was wearin' a dark gray suit with little white stripes. I think them folks back east calls it a pin stripe. Anyway, he had on a fancy white shirt that had somethin' akin ta lace on the front. More like ruffles, if'n yah asked me. He wore a red vest, too.

He sorta struck me as one of them riverboat gamblers, but there weren't no riverboats 'round these parts. Hell, the closest thin' we had ta a river 'round here was a creek that didn't have 'nough water in it ta float a canoe.

As the game progressed, I noticed the little fella would shake his head just a little from time to time. 'N other times, he would nod just a bit. Not so much as ta make it noticeable, unless you was watchin' him pretty close. Since he seemed ta be watchin' the gambler fella more than the others, I got ta thinkin' that maybe they had somethin' goin' on between 'um.

I took a minute ta think back about those two. I could remember the day that dude come ta town. It was hard ta forget. We don't get many duded up fellas like him 'round here. He took a room over at the hotel and pretty much kept ta his self for the better part of two days.

A couple a days later, the short little fella shows up. He took a room at the hotel, too. I remember seein' them at the hotel eatin', but they didn't sit tagether. As best I recollect they didn't talk between 'um selves, either. It didn't seem like they know'd each other.

Yesterday evenin', after the short little fella arrived, they sat down at different tables in the saloon and played a little poker with some of the local folks, and a few outta towners. They won a little and lost a little like most folks who play fair do.

They got the game they was a playin' tagether now earlier in the day. The two playin' with 'um were the two that won the most last night. That got me ta thinkin' there might be somethin' goin' on here I aught ta be lookin' for, but I weren't sure what it might be.

I took a quick look 'round the table at the money. It didn't seem ta me like there was much on the table. But after watchin' for a bit, I noticed every once 'n a while the short little fella would take a little money from in front of him off the table. He'd kinda careful like slipped it in his coat pocket. I looked over at the fancy dude just as he was doing the same thin'.

Then it hit me as ta what them fellas was up to. By takin' a little of their winnin's off the table at a time, they was makin' it look like they weren't winnin' all that much. I know'd for a fact a big pile of money in front of one player tends ta draw attention ta that player. It also tends ta get the others ta wonderin' if maybe he might be cheatin'.

Well, it got me to thinkin' they might be workin' tagether. They might also be doin' a bit a cheatin', too.

I took ta watching the little fella pretty darn close. Now I ain't no stranger to a deck of cards, but I have ta admit he was smooth. He could palm a card with the best of 'um.

Now I could've done somethin' about it right then and there, but I wanted ta see what the dude was doing, too. I watched the dude for a bit and noticed every time he got his hands on them cards, he seemed ta come up with a winnin' hand. Now the odds of that happenin' every time was pretty darn slim.

I thought I'd seen everythin' 'til now, but that dude was the smoothest fella I can ever remember with a deck of cards. It took me a while ta realize that he could deal off the bottom of the deck, palm a card, or pick one up without anyone knowin' what he was a doin'. The only reason I could tell what he was a doin' was I didn't have anyone else ta watch. I didn't have cards of my own ta keep an eye on. I could concentrate on every move that dude made.

Well, I sat there for a bit wonderin' if I should do somethin' about the cheatin', or if I should let them other darn fools lose their money to 'um. Bein' as I was the law, and it was agin' the law ta cheat at gamblin', I decided I better put a stop to it.

I got up and walked across the room ta the table. That dude fella, he glanced up at me when I stopped next to him. He was a smilin' from ear ta ear, that is until I sorta pulled my coat back away from my gun. It was then that he saw the shiny star pinned on my vest.

"Gentlemen, this here game is over," I said calm like so as not ta get anyone too riled up.

"What's the matter, Sheriff?" the cowboy said lookin' up at me.

"I've been watchin' this here game for some time now. The dude here, and that little fella across the table, have been cheatin'."

The cowboy looked at me. He was surprised at what I'd said. The look on his face told me that he didn't like the idea of some dude takin' him for his hard earned wages by cheatin'.

All of a sudden that cowboy pushed back his chair and started ta draw his gun as he stood up. It didn't take no education at tall ta know what was about ta happen.

I quickly drew my gun and laid the barrel along side that cowboy's head. He folded up like an old newspaper tossed on the floor. I turned my gun on the dude before he could do anythin' his self.

"I wouldn't do nothin' foolish if'n I was you," I said lookin' him in the eye.

The dude, he slowly took his hand out from inside his fancy coat. I guess he had no wish ta die right then 'n there. He would've, too, if'n he'd pulled anythin' out from under that coat 'cept'n his empty hand.

I reached inside his coat and pulled out a small little gun that weren't much more than a peashooter.

"I'll take this for safe keepin'. You got any other guns?"

The dude, he looked a might bit upset with me, but I guess he thought better of givin' me a hard time. That .45 Colt of mine tends ta make people more obligin'.

Slowly, he reached down and pulled up his pant leg and took a derringer out of his boot along with a knife. He also removed a derringer from up the sleeve of that fancy coat. He had more guns on him than the Army. There was also a few cards up his sleeves.

"Now, put both hands on the table where I can see 'um."

I then turned ta the little fella. I pointed my gun at him. There was no doubt in his mind I had him dead ta rights. He done let out a sigh that told me that he was plannin' on givin' up without a fight.

"Your turn. Very careful like put all your weapons on the table," I said.

"You mean, he was cheatin', too?" the drummer man asked.

"They was in this tagether from what I could see. Yah see, it didn't matter a hoot which one of 'um won the hand you was playin'. The money went inta the same pot at the end of the day. I 'spect they was goin' ta divvy it up later."

"Well, I'll be darned," the drummer man said. "What happens now?"

"I'll get these two locked up, then I'll decide how much of this money goes ta you and the cowboy. That is, after I take out 'nough to cover their fines."

"You can't do that," the dude objected.

"When yah cheat in my town, you pay the price. So let's get a move on. On your feet."

After I gathered up the money, I started them toward the door of the saloon. I was almost ta the door when the drummer man called out ta me.

"What about this young man?" he asked as he pointed to the cowboy lyin' on the floor.

"Well, from the looks of him, he ain't goin' no wheres."

"You hit him pretty hard, Sheriff."

I looked at the cowboy and had to agree. I had hit him hard, but it was a darn sight better than gettin' killed.

"You stay with him. I'll be back shortly ta take a look at him," I said, then headed out of the saloon with my prisoners.

As I took my prisoners across the street ta the jail, they commenced ta arguin'. It seemed the little guy was blamin' the dude for usin' fancy tricks ta cheat. The dude was blamin' the little guy for not keepin' his eyes on what was goin' on 'round 'um. It didn't take much for me ta see what they was a doin'. They was tryin' ta get me distracted.

I'd been sheriffin' for a long time. It weren't about ta work on me. I let them get a little further ahead of me than I would normally do. When they suddenly turned 'round, I was too far back for 'um ta get ta me without at least one of 'um endin' up dead.

As the dude turned, I jerked my gun up and pulled back the hammer. Now that gun of mine makes a powerful statement when the hammer clicks back. And with that .45 caliber barrel starin' him right in the face, he decided it was best if he didn't try anythin' stupid.

"Now if you're lookin' ta see if you can take me, I suggest you think about that. I'd as soon shoot you now as ta put up with you," I said as I watched the sweat start ta run down the dude's face.

"I ain't goin' ta give you no trouble," the little fella said as he put his hands in the air.

Not the dude, he was different. I could see by the look in his eyes that he had a powerful hate for me. I guess he didn't like me much for takin' his money.

"You got somethin' ta say to me?" I asked kinda quiet like as I held my gun so it was pointed at his face.

"No."

"If'n you don't turn 'round and march yourself ta that there jail, you'll wish you'd never seen this town," I said.

He turned 'round and walked ta the jail. I locked him in one of the two cells I had in the jail. I then locked the little fella in the other one.

I then went over ta my desk and put the money on it. I commenced ta countin' the money I done took off the gambler and his friend. It was a tidy sum, over four hundred dollars.

Now I'd been 'round long 'nough ta know that cowboys don't make a lotta money. But a good share of this here cash had come from the cowboy. He had won a tidy sum last night playin' agin' these fellas when the game was fair. The more I got ta thinkin' on it, the more I figured that the cowboy, and probably the drummer, had been set up for the game they was a playin' today. Let 'um win one night and then take 'um for everythin' they got the next. Kind of a neat setup, if'n you ask me.

"Well, I think I'll take your fines out of what I got here and give the rest to the cowboy and the drummer," I said after I turned 'round and looked at them two sittin' in my jail.

"You can't do that," the dude said as he stood up and looked out of the cell at me.

"You can't do that without a trial first," the little fella insisted.

"You want a trial?"

"Yes. Yes we do," the dude said.

"Fine. You will be the guest of the county for somewheres close to two 'n a half weeks, maybe a mite more."

"Two and a half weeks?" the little fella said with surprise.

"Yup. It will be at least two 'n a half weeks before the circuit judge will get 'round ta getting' here. Maybe a mite longer."

"You can't hold us here that long for cheating," the dude insisted.

"Say, you're the fellas that wants a trial."

I watched as they kinda looked at each other. I could hear them whisperin', but I couldn't understand 'um. I could get the gist of what they was talkin' 'bout though. I got the idea that neither of them wanted to hang around here that long.

"Say, Marshall,"

"Sheriff," I corrected the dude.

"Ah, yeah, Sheriff. What's the penalty if we decide not to have a trial?"

"Well, it's a hundred dollar fine, each that is, repayment of all funds to them fellas you cheated as best I can figure, and a day in jail. After that, I run you outta town. You can cheat all you want somewhere's else."

"What's most likely to happen if we wait for the judge?" the little fella asked.

"Well, the last fella, he got fined two hundred dollars and three months in jail, but longer in jail if'n you can't pay the fine. So I 'spect you'd get 'bout the same. You got 'nough money ta pay the fines and still pay back them's you cheated."

I watched them fellas as they took a minute ta look at each other. I could see they was a thinkin' pretty hard on what I'd just told 'um. I was sure they was thinkin' a day in jail and a hundred dollar fine didn't sound so bad after all.

"I gots to make 'rangements for you two ta eat. I'll be back in a few minutes," I said as I stood up.

I went on across the street ta the saloon ta check on the cowboy. When I got there he was a sittin' in a chair holding his head. He looked up when he saw me come in.

"You didn't have ta hit me so hard, Sheriff."

"You was about ta do somethin' that was goin' ta get you in a heap more trouble than a knot on the head. Now I want ta know how much money you come inta that game with taday?"

"About a hundred dollars," he said.

"Where'd you get a hundred dollars?"

"I just got paid for a cattle drive up from Texas, but I won most of the money yesterday agin' them two."

"Okay. If'n I give you a hundred and twenty dollars, you goin' ta be satisfied with that?" I asked hopin' that I'd knocked some sense inta his head when I hit him."

"I guess that's okay, but what about them gamblers?"

"You don't worry none about them. I'll take care of 'um. There's one more thin'. You gots to leave town."

"Okay, Sheriff," the cowboy agreed.

I counted out a hundred and twenty dollars from the money the gambler and his friend had and gived it ta the cowboy.

"Now, get on your horse and get a movin'. I don't want to see you 'round here in an hour."

The cowboy nodded that he understood what I was a tellin' him. He wasted no time, no time at tall pickin' up the money and gettin' out the saloon door.

As soon as he was gone, I went lookin' for the drummer. The Barkeep told me that he had gone ta the stage station ta wait for the stage. Sure 'nough, that's where I found him.

"You leavin' town?" I asked.

"Yes, sir, as soon as the stage gets here. I got no money, but I still got my ticket for the stage."

"Okay, but I got some of your money back for yah," I said. "How much did you lose ta those two?"

"About a hundred dollars, I guess."

"Okay. Here yah go," I said as I started countin' out a hundred dollars. "Make sure you get on that there stage."

"Yes, sir" he said as he put the money in his coat pocket.

I nodded, then turned 'round and headed back ta the jail.

When I got back ta the jail, I sat down at the desk and turned 'round to face the cells.

"Now, I gots forty dollars left here. I'm goin' ta give each of yah twenty dollars. Come sun up, I'm goin' to let you out of them cells. Within an hour of that time, I want you out of town. You understandin' what I'm a tellin' you?"

"Yes, sir," they replied together.

The drummer caught the stage onta the next town and the cowboy, he left town like he said. Come mornin', I let the dude and the little fella out of jail. The last I seen of 'um, they was hoofin' it on down the road and mighty glad ta be outta my jail and out of my town.

# THE LOST WAGONS

Three wagons had been moving west across the open prairie of the Dakota Territory, but had stopped because of the weather. The weather had been getting worse with each passing hour. The winds were increasing with strong gusts that caused the canvas tops on the covered wagons to flutter. The temperature had been steadily dropping all day. The sudden change in the weather had made movement difficult for both man and beast.

The small band consisted of Jacob Miller, his wife, Mary, and their two young sons in the lead wagon. Jacob was the self-appointed leader because he was the only one who had been out to the Dakota Territory before. Jacob was a strong Irishman with a short temper.

Isaac Waterman and his wife, Wilma, were in the second wagon. He was tall and slim, and had been a teacher in the east. His wife, Wilma, was a quiet little woman. They had no children and were on their way to teach in Deadwood.

Henry McAdams, his wife Beth, and their children were in the third wagon. Henry was a shy, quiet man. His wife was the one who made most of the decisions. It had been her idea to go west, not Henry's. He had made a good living making saddles and harnesses in Kentucky. Becky was fifteen and Billy was thirteen.

"What do you think, Jacob?" Isaac asked as he looked up at the gray sky.

"I don't rightly know. I ain't never seen it like this 'fore, 'specially this early in the season."

"You think we should hold up some wheres," Henry asked softly, not wanting to cause any trouble.

"Just where you suggestin' we hold up?" Jacob asked sharply. "Do you see anywheres we can get out of this here wind?"

"No," Henry replied shyly as he looked down at the ground.

"There's no need to get sharp with each other. We need to work together," Isaac said.

"Well, we ain't got enough wagons to make a circle, so the next best thin' is to brin' 'em up close to each other, the two heaviest wagons on the outside," Jacob suggested.

"Might I suggest that we put the wagons in sort of a U shape with the open end away from the wind," Isaac suggested. "That would make it possible for us to put the oxen in the middle. We could tie some ropes across the open end between the wagons to keep them from wondering off."

"That's a good idea," Henry agreed, but Henry often agreed rather than cause a confrontation.

"That might work," Jacob said thoughtfully. "We best get at it 'fore it gets any worse."

Isaac and Henry nodded in agreement as to what they were going to do and went to work. Everyone pitched in to make sure things were secure.

They had no more than finished arranging the wagons when it began to snow. With the wind, the snow was blowing in side ways. It instantly made it impossible to see. Huddled in their own wagons, they bundled up in blankets and quilts to keep warm.

The wind blew unceasingly for hours and the snow pelted the wagons. The temperature continued to drop. Darkness settled over the small band of travelers.

When morning came, the wind had died down to a gentle breeze and the snow had changed to light flurries. Jacob was the first to look outside. All he could see was a vast sea of white. When he looked inside the U formed by the wagons, all he could see was snow. It took a few seconds for Jacob to realize that the oxen were gone.

He tried to understand the situation they were in and think about what to do about it. Without the oxen, they were stranded. There was no way to move the heavy wagons without them.

Jacob jumped down off the back of the wagon and looked around. The wind had caused the snow to drift around the wagons causing high drifts that tapered off toward the south.

"Isaac, Henry, get out here," Jacob called as he looked out across the prairie in the hope of seeing the oxen.

Within a few minutes the three men were standing at the back of one of the wagons. The thought of being left without oxen to pull the heavy wagons was sinking in.

"The oxen are gone," Henry said when he jumped down from his wagon and look at the space were the oxen should have been.

"No kiddin'," Jacob replied sarcastically.

"Where do you think they might have gone?" Isaac asked as he joined the other two.

"Don't know for sure, but I 'spect they done went lookin' for a place to get out of the wind," Jacob replied.

"What do we do?" Henry asked, the sound of his voice showing he was afraid.

"Should we go look for them?" Isaac asked Jacob.

"Got no choice. We ain't goin' anywheres without 'um."

"Do you think it's a good idea for all of us to go? Shouldn't someone stay close to the wagons?" Isaac asked.

"I think that's a good idea," Henry said.

"It was a question. It weren't no idea. Besides we wouldn't have to go lookin' for them if'n you'd a tied your end of them ropes like you was told," Jacob said angrily.

"It's a little late to be blaming anyone," Isaac said.

"Maybe, but it's his fault them critters ain't here now," Jacob added.

"Spending time blaming one another isn't going to get them back. We need to decide how to get the oxen back."

It was decided that Jacob and Henry would go look for the oxen. Since the wind had been out of the north, it was felt they would have gone off with the wind at their backs.

Jacob and Henry spread out to about a hundred feet apart and then started to move south. As they moved out across the prairie, Jacob began to grumble to himself. It ate at him that Henry had not tied the ropes securely to the wagons. The further they went, the angrier Jacob became.

They had gone over two miles from the wagons when Henry suddenly dropped out of sight. Jacob could hear him calling for help, but couldn't see him. He carefully moved toward where he thought Henry's cries for help were coming from, but it wasn't until he was only a few feet away that he saw Henry. Henry had stepped off into a deep ravine that had been blown over with snow.

"Help me," Henry cried looking up at Jacob.

Jacob stood there looking down at Henry without moving. He was afraid that he might end up falling into the ravine, too. Jacob took a minute to look around. That was when he saw something, the tail of an ox sticking out of the snow.

Jacob quickly realized what had happened to the oxen. During the storm, the oxen had wondered off looking for shelter from the wind and the snow. They found shelter in the ravine and gathered in the bottom of it for protection, but the blowing wind and snow had turned it into a death trap.

"I should leave you there," Jacob yelled angrily.

Henry looked at him. He knew Jacob could do it. Without help, there was no chance Henry would be able to dig his way out. He was in it up to his neck and his movement in an effort to free himself had packed the snow tighter around him. He was getting cold and if he didn't get out soon, he would freeze to death.

"Help me, please. Don't leave me here."

To Jacob's way of thinking, he was looking at the man who might be responsible for the death of all of them.

As Jacob looked around, he could see Henry's tracks in the snow were slowly disappearing. The light snow blowing across the ground was filling in their tracks. In a little while Henry's tracks would disappear completely and no one would know where he had disappeared.

Jacob looked down at Henry one last time before he turned around and started to walk back the way he had come. He could hear Henry yelling for him to come back, but Jacob shut out Henry's cries for help.

Jacob began to realize his tracks were rapidly disappearing, too. He started to run back toward where he thought the wagons should be. It seemed to him that he had run for a long time, longer then it should have taken for him to find the wagons.

Running had caused Jacob to sweat under his heavy coat. When he realized he was lost, he stopped to look around. He tried to think, but all he could feel was the cold that chilled his sweaty body.

Jacob began to turn around and around in an effort to find something that would let him know which way to go. He soon discovered no matter which way he looked, everything looked the same. There was nothing but a sea of white.

He looked down at the ground near his feet. His own tracks where disappearing before his eyes. He had not realized the wind had picked up and it had turned into a ground blizzard.

Jacob was lost. The only thing he could do was to keep moving in order to keep from freezing to death.

Jacob started walking, but he knew if he didn't find some point of reference soon he would most likely end up walking around in circles. He had no idea where he was going or what was ahead of him. All he knew was if he stopped, he would freeze to death.

With the wind and snow, he was unable to see where he was going. He never saw the deep ravine as he walked over the edge. He fell into the ravine and struck his head on a rock. In a way, he had been luckier than Henry. He had died almost instantly, while Henry died a much slower death.

Back at the wagons, Isaac paced back and forth. He was looking out over the vast ocean of white, hoping to see Jacob and Henry returning with the oxen. Deep down, he knew there was little chance of finding the oxen. The animals could have gone in any direction, and there was no telling how far.

As the day slowly went by the wind began to pick up again and the snow seemed to have increased. It was hard to see anything. Isaac had already accepted the fact that Jacob and Henry were not likely to return. After he told the others, he climbed back in his wagon to get warm.

That night he could hear the cries of the families of Jacob and Henry. Isaac held his wife close to him. He had to wonder if any of them would survive.

When morning came, Isaac looked up at the canvas over the top of his wagon. There was no movement and he could not hear the wind blowing. He scrambled out from under the covers to the back of his wagon and looked outside. The brightness of the morning sun on the snow almost blinded him. He quickly pulled his head back inside the wagon.

"The sun is shining," he said excitedly to Wilma.

"Will you go looking for Jacob and Henry?" she asked, the look on her face indicating she didn't want him to leave.

"Maybe, but I'm sure I will find them both dead."

"What are we going to do without oxen to pull the wagons?"

"I don't know. I haven't thought that far ahead. I need to get up. There is a lot I have to figure out."

"We need to find something to eat."

"Yes, I agree. That is the first thing we must do."

Isaac quickly got himself ready to go out. As he jumped down off the back of the wagon, he looked around. The sky was a deep blue without a cloud in it. He could feel the warmth of the sun on his face. The air was still for the first time in days.

Isaac climbed under his wagon and took out several buffalo chips from a net hung under the wagon. He took the dry ones and built a fire in between the wagons. He gathered up a couple of pots and filled them with snow to melt so he could make coffee.

It wasn't long before everyone was up and had gathered around the fire. Each of them brought something to the fire so they all could eat. There was much to be done and many decisions to be made.

"I'm sorry to have to say this, but I doubt very seriously that Jacob and Henry are alive," Isaac began.

"How do you know that," Beth said defiantly.

"I don't really know, but think about it. They went off yesterday morning. It was very cold and the weather turned bad after they left. No one could survive without shelter out there."

"I don't know about the rest of you, but I need to know what happened to Henry," Beth said.

"I don't think we should wonder around out there looking for them," Wilma said quietly.

"My husband knew how harsh this country could be. He knew what we were getting into before we left. He knew this could happen," Mary said as she began to sob.

"I don't care what the rest of you are going to do, but I'm going looking for my father," young Billy McAdams said sharply.

"I don't think that is a good idea, Billy," Isaac said. "Your mother and sister need you now more than ever."

"Then what do you suggest we do. Stay here and die?" Beth asked, as anger and sadness seemed to fill her thoughts.

"No, but I do think we have a lot to do if we are going to get out of this alive."

"What are you suggesting? Are you suggesting we just go off and leave our husbands out there?" Beth asked angrily.

"In a way, yes," Isaac said softly. "They are dead, I'm sure of that. There is nothing we can do about that. We have to think about ourselves now."

"I will not forget him," Beth said sharply.

"I didn't say to forget him. All I'm saying is that we have to survive."

Beth looked at Isaac with hatred in her eyes. She was not about to be told what to do by some tall skinny schoolteacher. She stood up and grabbed her son by the arm and walked back to their wagon.

Isaac sat by the fire as he watched her. She got a gun from inside the wagon. With her son at her side, she started off across the prairie in the direction Henry had gone.

"Aren't you going to stop her, Isaac," Wilma asked.

"No."

Wilma said nothing more. She knew her husband was right. It was not wise for them to go too far from the wagons, but what could he do about it?

Isaac looked over at Becky McAdams. She was watching her mother and brother. He wanted to say something to her, but had no idea what he could say to her that would be of comfort.

"What do you think we should do?" Mary Miller asked of Isaac.

"I don't know, yet."

"Could I make a suggestion?" Mary asked shyly.

"Certainly. What's on your mind?"

"We all set out to go to Deadwood to make it our home. I think we should still do that," Mary said confidently.

"You want to go on?" Wilma asked, a bit surprised at the little woman's determination.

"Yes. None of us have anything to return to, and I have two young boys that need a place to grow up," Mary said.

Wilma looked Mary in the eyes. She could see the woman's determination and admired her for it.

"I believe we can do it if we put our minds to it," Wilma said as she reached out and put her hand on Isaac's arm.

Isaac looked at his wife, then at Mary. If the two of them were so sure it could be done, then it probably could be.

"We will have to leave a lot of things behind. Are you ready to travel light?" he asked.

"Yes," Mary said as she pulled her shoulders back and stood up straight.

"We could make a hand cart out of one of the wagons to carry what we need. It will take all of us to do it," Isaac said thoughtfully.

Mary, Wilma, Becky, the two young boys and Isaac began unloading all the items in the wagons. All the blankets and quilts were put in one wagon that would serve as a place where everyone could sleep while they were getting things ready. Another wagon was filled with what food they had and all the tools.

The third wagon they began to take apart, piece-by-piece. It was stripped down to the axles. Then they began to rebuild it and turn it into a handcart three or four people could pull. Isaac had seen such carts and knew they were used in this country and in other countries of the world.

Just before nightfall, Mary was looking out over the prairie and thinking about her husband being out there. She caught sight of something moving in the distance.

"Isaac, look," she said as she pointed off to the south.

Isaac and Wilma had been cutting on the boards from the wagon. They stopped and looked in the direction Mary was pointing. It wasn't long before they realized they were seeing Beth and Billy coming toward them. It was a relief to see them, although they had given up hope of ever seeing them again.

"We found Jacob and Henry," Beth said with a note of sadness in her voice. "You were right, Isaac, they are both dead. They died trying to get the oxen out of a snow drift."

"Did you see the oxen?" Isaac asked.

"Yes. They are all dead."

"Do you think you could find them again?"

"Yes," Beth replied, looking at Isaac as if he was asking something very strange.

"Good. In the morning, I want you to show me where they are. We will need meat. We might as will get some good out of them before they spoil in the sun."

"I'm not going back there," she said. "We buried Jacob and Henry there," she said defiantly.

"I'll take you there," Billy said as he looked at Isaac.

"What's been going on here? You've taken everything out of our wagon. What do you think you're doing?"

"We were not sure you would return. The rest of us decided we are going on."

"You decided? What gave you the right to make any decisions around here?"

"You were not here to consult. We're making a cart we can pull. We will be taking with us only those things we absolutely need and nothing more," Isaac explained.

"I won't leave my things behind," Beth insisted, the tone of her voice sharp and angry.

"Fine, then you can stay here with them," Isaac said, then turned around and walked away.

"Who does he think he is?" Beth said under her breath.

"Someone who is trying to save all of us," Mary replied sharply. "If you want to come with us, you can. But you had better do your part or you will be left behind. It will take the help of everyone just to survive."

"You can't do that," Beth said angrily.

"We can and we will," Wilma assured her, then turned and followed her husband.

Beth watched as Wilma and Mary walked toward the fire and started to fix dinner. She was angry, but she was also upset with the way she had been treated. She had never had anyone put her in her place before.

She looked at her son, Billy. He was standing there looking at her. From the expression on his face, she got the impression he was looking at a stranger.

"We'll show them," she said as she stepped toward her son.

"We'll show them what? They are right, you know," he said.

"What?"

"They are right. If we are to survive, we have to work together, all of us. Mr. Waterman is only trying to keep us all alive until we can get where we're going."

Billy turned and walked over to the fire. He walked up to Isaac and touched his arm. Isaac turned and looked down at the young boy.

"I'll take you to where the oxen are," he said.

Isaac looked at the boy and smiled. He then looked up and saw Beth. The look on her face was one he had hoped not to see. He was sure she felt as if he was turning her children against her.

Nothing more was said that evening. In the morning, Isaac and Billy went out to where the oxen were. They took their knives and cut off large chunks of the meat and carried it back to the wagons.

Mary and Wilma went to work to prepare some of the meat for travel, and cooked up the rest so it would last as long as possible. Every once in a while, Wilma would look up and see Beth sitting in her rocking chair next to her fancy dresser. Beth was not helping and it did not set well with Wilma or the others, including Beth's teenage daughter, Becky.

Meanwhile, young Billy joined in with the rest of them to help build the cart. Beth was hurt deeply by her children joining in to help, but there was nothing Billy could do about it. Isaac needed all the help he could get.

It took them several days to get the cart built and ready for travel. Since there was no wood to be found out on the prairie, the young children had the job of finding buffalo chips for the fire. The older children would gather snow to melt for water and fill the water barrels.

The weather had improved a great deal. Most of the snow had melted and the ground had dried. The dry ground would make it easier to pull the cart.

Isaac knew the heavier the cart, the more difficult it would be to pull. Only those things that would be needed every day would be loaded on the cart. Everything else would be left behind.

When morning arrived on the day they were to leave, the sun was shining and there was a gentle breeze out of the south. Isaac was the first one up. Mary and Wilma made a hearty breakfast for everyone.

Almost everyone had pitched in and had done their part. The only one who had been a source of contention was Beth. She had not done a thing to help.

Isaac walked over to Beth. He wanted her to say something, but she remained silent as she had since she returned from burying her husband.

"I know you're hurting, but it would be best if you would at least do your part."

"You've turned my children against me. Why should I help you?" she said bitterly.

"I have done nothing. They chose to join in. They only want to survive. Will you join us?"

"No. I hope you all die out there. I'm staying here with my husband and my things," she said glaring at him.

"I will not force you to come with us. We need all the help we can get. We don't need to carry someone else's weight because they are too stubborn to even want to live. You are welcome to stay here."

Isaac looked at her for a minute, then turned and walked back to the fire. Everyone was sitting around eating.

"Aren't you going to take her something to eat?" Isaac asked of the two women who were cooking.

"I will not take her anything. She has not lifted a single finger to help. I have taken a plate of food to her for the last time. If she can't come over here and get it herself, she can go hungry," Mary said.

"Wilma? What about you?"

"I'm sorry, Isaac. I can't."

"I understand,"Isaac conceded.

Nothing more was said, and no one took anything to her. They busied themselves getting the cart ready to leave.

When all was ready, Isaac took his place at the center of the cross bar on the tongue of the cart. He took a quick look back at Beth, shook his head and then gave the order to pull.

The cart lunged forward and started to move. Once the cart was moving, it moved slowly but steadily. The big wagon wheels made it a little easier for the cart to roll over bumps in the ground.

The going was slow, but they were making progress toward the Black Hills. It was not easy moving the cart. During the first day, they managed to travel about ten miles from where they had left the other wagons. They set up camp using the tarps from two of the wagons to make tents to sleep in. It had been a quiet day as no one wished to speak of leaving Beth McAdams behind.

"Isaac?"

"Yes, Wilma"

"I was wondering, . . . ," she said, then paused as if she was reconsidering what she wanted to say.

"What is it, dear?" Isaac insisted.

"Do you think Beth might come with us now that she has spent the day alone?"

"I don't know. What are you suggesting?"

"I was thinking maybe you could make one last attempt to get her to come along?" she asked, her eyes pleading with him to understand how she was feeling.

"You want me to go all the way back and try to convince her that she should come with us. Is that right?"

"Yes," she replied with a smile.

Isaac didn't like what she was asking him to do. He looked down at the ground and thought about it. The way he figured it, he would have to travel twenty miles for nothing if she still refused to come with him. It would also cause at least a day's delay, probably two before he could get back, and she might not want to come anyway. He could not see where it was going to do any good. Beth was as stubborn a woman as he had ever met.

He decided that he had to have the agreement of the majority of the group. It was only fair since they were going to be delayed at least a day, maybe more.

"I would like everyone to gather around the fire," Isaac called out, then waited for them all to settle down.

"I have been asked to go back and try to convince Beth to come and join us," he said without emotion.

He could hear a few groans from some of those gathered around the fire.

"Who asked you?" Becky asked.

"That's not important. The decision we must make is, do I go back and try to get her to come along or do we go on?"

"I think you have done everything you could to get her to come with us. She made her choice. Now she should have to live with it," Billy said.

"I agree," Becky said. "Even if she changes her mind and decides she will come along, will she do anything to help or will we have to carry her load as well?"

"I don't think she will come if you go back to get her. I think it's a waste of time," Mary said. "I hate to have left her out there alone, but she asked for it."

"I agree, she asked for it," Wilma said. "But do you really want to leave her out there to die?"

"No," Billy replied, "but she's the one who made the decision to stay behind."

"Okay," Isaac said. "At first light, we will take a vote. If the vote of the majority is I go back and try to get her to join us, then I will. But if the vote is to go on without her, that is what we will do. Is that fair enough?"

The group as a whole really didn't want to vote on such a matter. Isaac had given them a way out, even if it was just for the night. They were all tired and most of them felt it was better if they voted on it in the morning when they would be better able to deal with it.

When morning came, they gathered around the fire. No one was willing to open the subject of going back to get Beth. It wasn't until most of them were finished with breakfast they realized Billy was gone.

"Where's Billy," Isaac asked Becky.

"He went to see if he could get mother to join us."

"I'd better go after him. I want you to break camp and move out. Leave us a good trail to follow and make at least five miles each day. We should be able to catch up in a couple of days," he instructed Wilma.

"Don't you think it would be best if we wait here?"

"No. Do as I say," Isaac insisted.

Isaac got together what he could so he could travel light. He needed to catch up with Billy as quickly as possible. Isaac kissed Wilma goodbye, then started out after Billy.

Billy had left an easy trail to follow. He was using the wheel tracks from the cart as a guide. Isaac's long legs helped him to cover ground rather quickly. It was only midday when he finally caught up with Billy.

Together they pressed on toward the place where they had left Billy's mother. When they arrived, they found Beth sitting in the rocking chair with her head tipped down. When she looked up at them, they could see the streaks on her face from tears.

"Mother," Billy called to her as he ran up to her and knelt down next to the rocking chair.

Isaac stood by and watched the tearful reunion. All he could think of was if this didn't get her to come with them, nothing would.

"Mrs. Miller, we have come back to get you. We want you to come with us. There is nothing you can do here. Won't you please come with us?" Isaac asked.

"Please, mother. Come with us."

She looked from her son to Isaac, then back at her son. Yesterday had proven to be the loneliest day of her life. She had not seen a soul after they had left. She had plenty of time to think. She had eaten a little, but only enough to stay alive.

"Yes, I will come with you," she finally conceded.

Billy jumped up and held out his hand. She took his hand, then started out walking with them.

The three of them walked along the trail left by the cart. Nothing was said, but it was clear she had had time to think about how she had acted. She prayed they would forgive her.

It took them three days to rejoin the others. Once they were together, she pitched in and helped in any way she could to make the trip easier. It was her way of trying to make up to them.

It was late October when the small band of travelers finally walked down the main street of Deadwood pulling the cart with all they owned. They were dirty and tired, but they had made it to Deadwood.

# THE CAPTURE OF
# "ONE EAR" BUTLER

I was on my way to the settlement of Deadwood to find and arrest a man who had escaped from the territorial prison at Fort Randall. His name was James Earl Butler, also known as "One Ear" Butler. I might add he was not called that to his face by anyone who wanted to live very long.

"One Ear" wasn't a very tall man, but he was stocky and very strong. He was a gunfighter with a mean streak as wide as his broad shoulders. He had a full beard and thick mustache, and carried a six-gun with mother of pearl pistol grips.

The story of how he got the name "One Ear" went something like this. It seems he got into a gunfight some years back with three men in Belle Fourche. One of them shot off a piece of his left ear.

After Butler killed two and wounded the third, he walked up to the wounded man and shot both the man's ears off before he killed him. I don't know how much of the story was true, but the story told me two things about Butler. It told me that he was as mean as they said he was, and it told me that he was pretty good with a gun.

It was getting on toward late afternoon when I saw smoke from a campfire. I reined up. Looking through my field glasses I could see two men at a campfire. One of them was squatting down next to the fire while the other was lying on the ground leaning back against his saddle.

After watching them for a few minutes, I decided I would ride up to their camp. I checked my pistol to make sure it was ready for use then checked my saddle rifle. I had no intention of riding into a trap without being prepared. I also took my badge off my shirt. There was no sense letting them know who I was before it was necessary.

I started to move closer to the camp. When I got close enough so they could see me, I called out.

"That coffee smells good. Mind if I ride in?" I shouted as I reined up.

The one leaning on the saddle turned his head a little and looked toward me, but he didn't get up. The one squatting next to the fire put his cup down and stood up.

"Come on in and sit a spell," the one leaning against the saddle said.

I nudged my horse forward, leading my pack horse along. I reined up and stepped out of the saddle. While keeping one eye on them, I tied my horses to a tree before I walked into their camp.

"Pour the man a cup of coffee, Billy."

Billy looked at me for a second before he squatted down next to the fire and poured a cup full of coffee. He then stood up and held the cup out to me.

"Much obliged," I said as I took the cup.

"Pull up a piece of that log. What's your handle?"

"I'm William Turnwell," I said as I sat down on a log.

"I'm James Butler and that's Billy McHenry."

The name of James Butler about knocked me off the log, but I doubt they noticed. I had not expected to run into him this far from Deadwood. I had to wonder if he was really the man I was looking for. He didn't look as stocky as I had been led to believe. I could not see the left side of his face, so I couldn't be one hundred percent sure.

The only other thing I knew that might help me identify the man was his gun. From where I was sitting I couldn't see the handgrips. It wasn't until he shifted around a little that I was able to see the mother of pearl handgrips.

"What you doing in these parts," Butler asked.

"I'm on my way to Deadwood."

"I think I've heard of you," Billy said as he studied my face for a minute.

"Oh, really?"

I was not sitting in the best position if things suddenly turned sour.

"I hear tell of a Turnwell over near Pickstown. That where you're from?" Billy asked, watching me rather closely.

He was looking for some kind of a reaction, but I didn't make a move. I did, however, notice he had not picked up his cup. He was standing flat footed and his hand was close to his gun.

"No."

"I think he was a Sheriff or Marshall."

"No kin of mine that I know of, but I'm from a pretty large family. Most of them in Tennessee, but I might have a kin up this way."

Billy seemed to be satisfied with my answer for the moment. He squatted back down next to the fire and picked up his cup. I knew there was still a chance something could go wrong.

"You got business in Deadwood?" Butler asked.

"I'm supposed to meet a man in Deadwood. We have some business to discuss," I replied, keeping my answer vague.

"We just come from there," Butler said.

"Oh. What's it like there? I've never been to Deadwood."

"Nice little place. They've got lots of women there," Butler said with a big grin.

"Sounds great."

"You lookin' to go on a piece yet today?" Billy asked, watching me over the top of his cup.

I got the impression Billy was not too willing to have me hang around. In fact, I was sure he would prefer I finish my coffee and get on my way.

"Hadn't given it much thought. I'm in no hurry."

"I thought you said you was meetin' someone in Deadwood." Billy said as his eyes narrowed slightly.

He was wanting me to leave for some reason. I had to wonder if he had figured out it was "One Ear" I was looking for, but I couldn't see how he could come to that conclusion.

Billy was pretty sure he had seen me before. I knew it was only a matter of time before he figured it out. I was hoping he would not be able to put it together for a little while longer.

"Billy, what's the matter with you?" Butler asked.

"Nothing boss. I just keep thinkin' I know this fella."

"Hell, Billy, you could've seen him almost anywhere. We've been all over," Butler said with a disgusted look on his face.

"You're welcome to spend the night here at our camp if'n you like," Butler said.

"I don't know," I said as I looked toward Billy. "If he's not comfortable with me here, I might as well move on. Besides, those girls in Deadwood sound mighty interesting."

Butler looked at Billy, then at me. I don't think he considered me much of threat to him, and that was in my favor. The one thing I did know was I had best come up with some idea as to how I was going to get Butler arrested.

"Billy, why don't you start fixing us some supper," Butler suggested. "You join us?"

"Well, I don't know. I don't think your friend likes me very much. Maybe it would be best if I go on my way."

I tried to make it sound as if it was no big deal. I didn't want to cause any discontent. Besides, I had been working on a plan in my head on how I was going to capture them. What I had been planning might work best if I were to leave.

"Well, suit yourself."

I drank down the last of my coffee and stood up. I took the cup over to Billy and handed it to him.

"Thanks for the coffee," I said with a smile.

Billy didn't say anything. He nodded as he looked up at me. I wasn't sure if he had been able to figure out where he had seen me before. I hoped he wouldn't for at least a while.

"Thanks for the hospitality. Maybe we'll meet again somewhere," I said as I looked at Butler.

"Maybe," he replied.

As I turned to walk back toward my horses, I noticed something I hadn't seen before. There was a dark spot on the blanket Butler had been laying on. There was also one on his pant leg. I thought it might have been blood. It looked as if it was still wet.

I had to wonder if Butler had been injured in a gunfight. All the time I was in their camp he never made an effort to get up. Billy had done everything that required movement.

As I pulled the reins to my horses loose from the tree, I glanced back toward the campfire. Billy was squatting down by the fire, but he was looking at me. Butler was still leaning back against the saddle watching me.

I put my foot in the stirrup and swung into the saddle. I reached up, tipped my hat and nodded to them. Billy watched me as I turned my horses and started off away from their camp.

As I rode away, I was tempted to turn around and look back at them, but I thought better of it. It was best they thought I was leaving.

There was a rise close to their camp where a body could see for some distance. I rode until I was well out of sight of anyone that might go up on the rise.

I passed over a hill and down the other side. When I got to the bottom of the hill, I turned and began working my way around the base of it. I did it for two reasons.

The first was so if they decided I was a threat to them, they would not find me camped on the other side of the hill. The second was so it would bring me around so I would be closer to their camp, only on a different side of them.

I had noticed a small hill off to the south of their camp. From there I would be able to see their camp with my field glasses. I would be able to watch them until dark. After dark, I could get closer and hopefully take them by surprise.

When I came to a place among some trees along a ravine, I stepped out of the saddle. I tied my horses to one of the trees. My horses began to graze and seemed comfortable there. I began working my way up to the top of the hill. At the top of the hill I laid down on the ground and watched what they were doing.

I don't know how long I watched, but I noticed Billy was still doing everything. That simply confirmed what I suspected. Butler had been injured.

I continued to watch until it was getting too dark to see anything other than their fire. It was time for me to get something to eat. It would give them time to settle down and go to sleep.

I went down the hill, built a small fire in the bottom of a ravine and cooked my dinner. Once I had finished, I sat back and drank coffee as I watched my fire slowly burn out.

It had been dark for some time when my fire finally went out. I looked up at the sky. It was clear and in a little while there would be a moon coming up over the horizon. There wouldn't be very much light from the moon, but there would be enough to help me find my way.

I climbed back up to the top of the hill and looked toward where Billy and Butler had been camping. I could see a fire, but it was too small to see what was going on around it. I would have to get a lot closer before I could see them.

With my rifle clutched tightly in my hand, I worked my way down the hill. It was slow going, but when I got closer I could see Billy was sitting with his back against a tree. It looked as if he was asleep, that is until he moved to put a stick on the fire. The fact that he was awake was going to make it more difficult for me to get to Butler. It meant I would have to take him out before I could get to Butler.

I worked my way around behind Billy. When I was only a few feet from Billy, I saw Butler move. I froze in my tracks. It was dark, but if he could see me in the moonlight it was over. I held my breath.

Butler simply rolled over a little and let out a deep sigh. I sensed he was not completely awake. From what little I could see of Billy, he was watching Butler.

I waited for everything to settle down again. As I was about to reach around the tree and grab Billy, he leaned forward. I pointed my gun at him and waited. He was putting another stick on the fire.

Again, I waited and watched. I felt the need to get it over with quickly. The longer I sat in the dark, the greater the chance one of them might get a glimpse of me. It was now or never.

As soon as Billy had leaned back against the tree again, I grabbed him. I stuck my gun against the side of his head as I reached around and put my free hand over his mouth. I half expected him to put up some kind of resistance, but he didn't make a move or a sound. I leaned up close to him.

"If you want to live to see the sun come up, don't make a sound," I whispered in his ear.

I didn't hear a thing, but all of a sudden Butler had his gun in his hand and there was a muzzle flash and the thunderous explosion of a gunshot. I felt Billy's body jerk and a muffled sound come from his mouth. I fired two quick shots at the place where the muzzle flash had come from as I scrambled for cover behind a log.

It was dead quiet in a couple of seconds. The only thing I could hear was my heart beating so I knew I was alive. I listened for sounds, any sounds at all. Since I was not sure if I had hit Butler, I laid still.

Slowly I raised my head and looked around the end of the log. There was so little light that I wasn't sure if Butler was still lying on the bedroll or not. Nothing was moving. I laid silently on the cool damp ground hoping for some movement or a sound that would give me some idea of where he was and what he was doing, but there was nothing.

Suddenly, there was a faint sound off to my right. It was close by, over where Billy laid. It sounded sort of like a movement in the grass, the slight rustle of leaves or the movement of dry grass.

I knew there was no way Butler could have gotten over to where Billy laid. It had to be Billy who was making the noise. Butler's shot must not have killed him.

I turned and looked back toward where I had seen Butler in time to see him shoot again. I raised my gun quickly and fired a shot at the muzzle flash. There was a loud groan, then I heard something fall on the ground.

I had hit Butler, but had I hurt him enough to put him down and keep him down. There was no way for me to tell in the dark. The only thing I could do was to wait.

Time passed slowly. I occasionally heard a slight moan from the other side of the campfire which had burned down to nothing but a few red coals. I also heard an occasional movement over near where Billy laid. I wanted to go help Billy, but I knew it might be the last thing I did, so I continued to wait.

The minutes passed into hours. Light was starting to show in the eastern sky. It would soon be light enough for me to see, but it would also make it light enough for Butler to see me. I waited.

It wasn't long and there was enough light for me to see the saddle Butler had been leaning on earlier, but there was no one there. I ducked back behind the log and tried to think. Where had he gone? Was he waiting for me to stick my head up?

It was then that I heard a groan. It was off to my left. Since Billy was off to my right I knew it wasn't him. I swung around in time to see Butler leaning against a tree. He was looking at me and had his gun in his hand. The look on his face showed me that he was in a great deal of pain. He started to raise his gun. I didn't wait.

I immediately fired a shot that hit him in the chest. He fell backwards and didn't move. I slowly got up, not taking my eyes off him. There was no doubt in my mind he was still a danger to me if he was alive.

Keeping my gun pointed at him, I moved closer. I could see his eyes looking up to the sky, but they weren't seeing anything. James Earl "One Ear" Butler was dead.

There were two bright red spots on his chest. It wasn't until I was almost standing over him that I saw the blood stain on his leg. He had been shot sometime earlier, by who I had no idea.

I remembered Billy. I turned around and walked over to where he had been. Billy had been shot in the gut. It had taken all night for him to die. From the looks of him, he must have died just minutes ago.

After I wrapped Butler and Billy in their bedrolls, I went and got my horses and brought them back to Butler's camp site. I put a few pieces of firewood on the coals and got the fire going again. After I finished eating my breakfast and put out the fire, I put Billy and Butler across their horses. I swung up into the saddle and began the long trip back to Fort Randall.

Once I returned to Fort Randall, I would collect the reward and settle back into the routine of keeping the peace in Pickstown. The one thing I knew for sure was I would not have to deal with "One Ear" Butler coming into Pickstown and starting trouble. But I also knew there were others out there who could be just as much trouble, maybe more.

# HARNEY PEAK HOTEL

Sam Jessup stepped out of the Harney Peak Hotel onto the large veranda after a good hearty meal. Sam was a tall man with a thick handlebar mustache and a full head of hair that flowed out from under his cowboy hat. The black pants he wore were tucked into the top of a pair of well-worn boots. He carried a .45 caliber Colt Peacemaker in a holster on his hip, and a .36 caliber Smith and Wesson tucked in his belt as a spare. On the black vest he wore over a white shirt was the silver star of a town marshal.

Marshall Jessup looked down Hill City's main street that was known as "One Mile of Hell". The street was called that because there was a church at each end of town with fifteen bars in between.

It was getting on toward dark when Marshall Jessup stepped off the veranda. This was the time of day he normally made his rounds of the local liquor establishments to see that peace was maintained.

When Sam reached the end of the street, he crossed to the other side and started working his way back toward the Harney Peak Hotel. Half way back to the hotel, he turned and walked into the Silver Dollar Saloon.

The Silver Dollar was more than just a saloon. It was also a brothel that was well known for the friendly women that worked there. Sam walked up to the bar and leaned against it as he looked around. He was looking for Kate, the owner of the saloon.

Kate was a pretty woman with blond hair that hung down to her shoulders in ringlets, a nice figure and a pleasant smile. She ran the Silver Dollar and had more than a passing acquaintance with Sam. It was fairly common knowledge around town that Sam and Kate were lovers, even though they tried to keep that fact between themselves.

Sam smiled as Kate walked up and leaned against the bar next him. She looked at him. Her eyes sparkled with her love for Sam.

"Evenin' Sam," she said, her voice soft and friendly.

"Evenin' Kate. Looks a bit quiet tonight," Sam said as he smiled at her.

"It's still early. Are you here to see someone, or you makin' your rounds?" she asked in a pleasant and sexy voice.

"Just makin' rounds, Kate," he replied.

"Will you be back later?"

"You can count on it."

"I'll be waiting for you," she said with a smile.

Sam gave her a wink, lightly touched her hand, then left the Silver Dollar Saloon.

After completing his rounds, he returned to the Harney Peak Hotel and sat down on a chair on the veranda. From there he could keep an eye on a good portion of the town.

The town was unusually quiet for a Saturday night. In fact, it was so quiet Sam accepted an invitation from a couple of the managers of the Harney Peak Mining Company to join them for a drink. They went inside the Harney Peak Hotel and sat down at a table in the lobby. One of the women working in the hotel got them drinks.

They were discussing the future of the town when a man stepped in the front door of the hotel, stood there and looked around. Sam took notice of the man, but didn't say anything. Instead, he simply looked him over.

The young man wore his gun low on his hip and tied down on his leg. There was little doubt in Sam's mind that the man thought of himself as a gunfighter. Sam wondered what he was doing in Hill City. The man turned and looked at him.

"You the sheriff of this here town?" the young man asked calmly and politely.

"I'm the town marshal. What can I do for yah?"

"You Sam Jessup?"

"Yeah. Who are you?"

"I'm Tom Putnam," he said as if Sam should know who he was.

"Do I know you?"

Sam looked Putnam over more closely this time. He couldn't remember having seen him before, but he got the impression it didn't really matter. Putnam didn't look like he was there to make a social call. There was something a lot more serious on Putnam's mind.

"I doubt it, but I've been lookin' for you for some time. My older brothers, George and

Paul, are down at the Silver Dollar. I've come down here to invite you to a killin'."

"Oh. Who you boys plannin' on killin'?" Sam asked calmly.

"We're plannin' on killin' you."

With that said, the others sitting around the table quickly stood up. Keeping their hands in plain sight so they didn't make the stranger nervous and accidentally cause a gunfight, they backed away from the table out of harm's way.

"Before we get to it, might I ask why? I think that's only fair since you plan on killing me, don't you?"

"Yeah, I guess so," Putnam said thoughtfully. "You might as well know why you're goin' ta die.

"Yeah, I think I'm entitled to know that."

"A few months back you killed our uncle over in Deadwood. You cut him down in the street with no warnin'."

"I think you got your facts a little mixed up, boy. He drew down on me first."

"That's what the sheriff said, but we didn't believe him none. My uncle was fast with a gun. I ain't never seen anyone that could beat him."

Sam was not stupid. He knew all too well this was not looking good for him. He could remember the man that had drawn on him in Deadwood. The guy had been fast, too fast. Although the man had been a might bit faster, Sam had been a darn sight more accurate.

Putnam had told him there were three of them gunning for him. It would be a lot better for Sam if he was in a position to put this one out of action before he had to face the other two. At the moment it didn't look like that was going to happen.

Since Sam was sitting down, he was at a big disadvantage. There was no way he could draw his gun without getting himself killed. He would have to wait and hope for a better opportunity.

"Since we ain't here to hurt no one but you, we'll meet you in the street out front."

"That's mighty obligin' of yah, but don't you think three against one is a might bit unfair?" Sam asked as he slowly stood up.

Sam was not the type of man to miss anything. He was a patient man who could wait for his opportunity. Putnam let his hand slide down next to his gun as Sam started to get up. It was clear that Putnam was ready to draw if Sam tried anything. Sam didn't make a move toward his gun.

"I think we're bein' real fair by lettin' yah know we're here. We could have bushwhacked yah whilst yah was makin' your rounds a little bit ago. But if'n you've a mind, we can settle it right now," he said confidently.

"Then let's settle it. It'll be just you and me right now, right here," Sam said.

Putnam glanced over at the other men that were standing around. He turned back and looked at Sam for a moment.

"They'll stay out of this," Sam assured him.

Sam didn't know anything about the young man, but it might be his only chance to avoid facing all three of them at once. Sam was sure by agreeing to settle with a one-on-one fight right now it would cause Putnam to lose his edge. Since Putnam hadn't seen the gunfight when his uncle had been killed, Sam was pretty certain Putnam would have some doubts creep into his mind about how fast Sam really was. That could help Sam when it came down to drawing against him.

Now it was Putnam's turn to be nervous. He had been called out in front of several of the town folks. To his way of thinking, it would be cowardly to refuse to have it out with the marshal. He had always thought his uncle was the fastest man with a gun, but suddenly he wasn't so sure. The fact that the marshal didn't seem to be the least bit afraid of him caused him to wonder if the marshal was as good with a gun as he had heard. He also wondered what the marshal was thinking.

Putnam began to sweat. Sam noticed Putnam wipe his hand on his pants. He also saw his fingers twitching nervously near the gun on his hip. This was not the first time Sam had seen a man react this way under pressure. He knew Putnam had become unsure of what he had gotten himself into. His inexperience was starting to cause him doubts.

Suddenly there were guns that seemed to jump out of holsters and into the men's hands. Two quick flashes and loud bangs instantly followed from the barrels of the guns. The air was filled with the thunder of guns going off and the smell of burnt gunpowder. Both men had been quick, but only one of them had hit his mark.

When the smoke cleared there was only one man standing. Putnam was lying on the floor. Sam's bullet had hit him square in the chest dropping him right where he stood. Putnam's gun was still in his hand and there was a large red spot on the front of his shirt. His eyes were open, but they were not seeing anything. Putnam had met his match and now he was dead.

Sam took a deep breath and let out a long sigh. He had been lucky. The kid was fast, but like his uncle he was not very accurate.

Sam looked around for a second, then walked over to the desk clerk. He knew he still had two others who wanted him dead, and now they would want him dead even more. He was going to need all the help he could get. He also knew he could not expect help from any of the town's citizens.

"Give me the scatter gun you keep under the counter."

The desk clerk knew it was not a request but a demand. To refuse might not be the best thing for him to do. He reached down and retrieved the shotgun and handed it to the marshal.

Sam was not about to waste any time. He wanted to get to the Silver Dollar Saloon before the remaining Putnam brothers got wind of the death of their younger brother. He had no more than stepped out the door of the Harney Peak Hotel when a shot rang out and pieces of wood flew into the air. The bullet had struck the veranda railing in front of him.

Sam swung around and saw a man in the middle of the street with a gun pointed in his direction. He instantly pulled the trigger on the shotgun and let loose with both barrels. The blast from the shotgun knocked the man down. He was lying on his back in the street looking up at the sky, but he was not seeing it. He, too, was dead.

As Sam walked into the street, he reloaded the shotgun. He stopped and looked down at the body. The man looked like a slightly older version of the young man he had shot a few minutes ago. He was obviously one of the Putnam brothers.

Several men came out on the street to see what had happened. It was only a matter of minutes before a crowd began to gather around in front of the mercantile store.

"Get him off the street," Sam ordered as he started to turn around.

"I see you're still alive," a voice called out from down the street.

The crowd moved away from Sam leaving him standing alone. Sam could see the man standing in the middle of the street had his feet firmly planted. He was in a position to draw against the marshal at any moment.

Sam moved toward the center of the street in front of the hotel. He still had the shotgun in his hands, but he knew it would be of little use now. The shotgun was a good short-range weapon, but it was not made for long distances.

"Which one are you?" Sam asked, keeping his voice as calm as he could.

"I'm George Putnam, and you're a dead man."

Sam knew the shotgun might reach out and put a couple of pellets in Putnam, but it wouldn't put him down. His only chance was to drop the shotgun and draw his pistol. There was one other thing of concern. This Putnam didn't seem to have the lack of confidence the other two had shown. This one was ready for a gunfight.

As far as Sam was concerned, there was no way out of it. That being the case, he saw no reason not to get it over.

Without making a move that would give Putnam even the slightest hint he was about to draw, Sam simply let go of the shotgun and drew his pistol in one smooth motion. His gun had cleared his holster before the shotgun even hit the ground, but he was not fast enough.

The sounds of two shots in quick succession went off, first Putnam's, then Sam's. Sam's luck had run out. Putnam's bullet caught Sam in the side, causing him to spin around and go crashing to the ground. When he hit the ground, he dropped his gun.

Sam's bullet hit Putnam in the left arm, but Putnam hardly even flinched. Seeing Sam down, Putnam began slowly walking toward him. There was hate in his eyes and a mean look on his face. There was little doubt he was going to finish Sam off.

Sam tried to crawl to his gun, but it was no use. The burning pain in his side clouded his head. On the verge of passing out Sam could hardly see Putnam, but he knew he was coming toward him.

Putnam walked up and looked down at Sam. He was only a few feet away as he looked at Sam. He slowly raised his gun.

"I want the last thing you see to be the flash of my gun as the bullet rips through your head," Putnam said angrily.

Suddenly there was the sharp report of a gun from behind Putnam. Putnam stiffened up and a shocked look came over his face. With his free hand, he tried to reach his back. The gun fell from Putnam's hand and dropped to the ground next to Sam. He staggered a few steps before he started to lean forward and fell flat on his face in the street.

Sam looked toward where the shot had come from and saw Kate with a gun held firmly in both hands. He then passed out.

Kate had several of the men standing around take Sam to a room in the Harney Peak Hotel. She dressed his wound and sat with him day and night for several days before he finally came around.

She spent the next few weeks nursing him back to health; feeding him, bathing him, and making sure he ate. While she looked after him, they talked about what the future held in store for them.

By the time Sam had recovered enough that he was able to return to work as the town marshal, Kate and Sam had decided it was time for both of them to move on and seek different work.

Kate sold the saloon to her barkeeper, and Sam quit his job as the town marshal. They married at the small Baptist Church at the edge of town before leaving Hill City for Wyoming where they built a ranch and raised a family. And as the story goes, they lived happily ever after.

* * * *

The Harney Peak Hotel still stands on the main street of Hill City, South Dakota, in the Black Hills. It looks very much like it did at the time of this story except that now it is a very well known restaurant visited by people from all over the world. The Harney Peak Hotel is now known as The Alpine Inn.

www.ingramcontent.com/pod-product-compliance
Lightning Source LLC
Chambersburg PA
CBHW071150170626
46809CB00002B/851